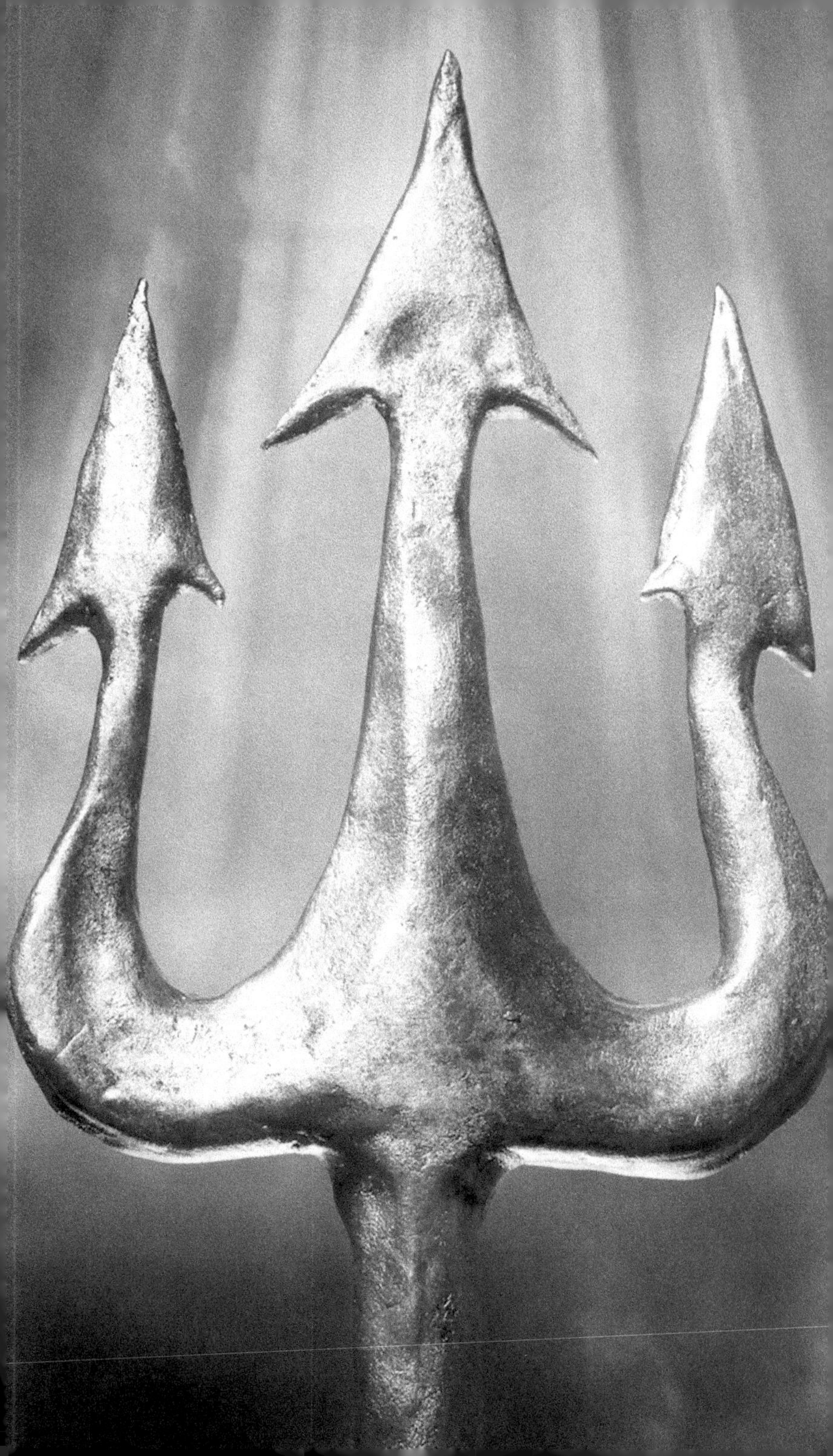

TORN in Half

Trident Security Book 12

SAMANTHA COLE

AUTHOR'S NOTE

The story within these pages is completely fictional but the concepts of BDSM are real. If you do choose to participate in the BDSM lifestyle, please research it carefully and take all precautions to protect yourself. Fiction is based on real life but real life is *not* based on fiction. Remember—Safe, Sane and Consensual!

Any information regarding persons or places has been used with creative literary license so there may be discrepancies between fiction and reality. The Navy SEALs missions and personal qualities within have been created to enhance the story and, again, may be exaggerated and not coincide with reality.

The author has full respect for the members of the United States military and the varied members of law enforcement and thanks them for their continuing service in making this country as safe and free as possible.

WHO'S WHO AND THE HISTORY OF
TRIDENT SECURITY & THE COVENANT

***While not every character is in every book, these are the ones with the most mentions throughout the series. This guide will help keep readers straight about who's who.

Trident Security (TS) is a private investigative and military agency, co-owned by Ian and Devon Sawyer. With governmental and civilian contracts, the company got its start when the brothers and a few of their teammates from SEAL Team Four retired to the private sector. The original six-man team is referred to as the Sexy Six-Pack, as they were dubbed by Kristen Sawyer, née Anders, or the Alpha Team. Trident had since expanded and former members of the military and law enforcement have been added to the staff. The company is located on a guarded compound, which was a former import/export company cover for a drug trafficking operation in Tampa, Florida. Three warehouses on the property were converted into large apartments, the TS offices, gym, and bunk rooms. There is also an obstacle course, a Main Street shooting gallery, a helicopter pad, and more features necessary for training and missions.

In addition to the security business, there is a fourth warehouse that now houses an elite BDSM club, co-owned by Devon, Ian, and their cousin, Mitch Sawyer, who is the manager. A lot of time and money has gone into making The Covenant the most sought after membership in the Tampa/St. Petersburg area and beyond. Members are thoroughly vetted before being granted access to the elegant club.

There are currently over fifty Doms who have been appointed Dungeon Masters (DMs), and they rotate two or three shifts each throughout the month. At least four DMs are on duty at all times at various posts in the pit, playrooms, and the new garden, with an additional one roaming around. Their job is to ensure the safety of all the submissives in the club. They step in if a sub uses their safeword and the Dom in the scene doesn't hear or heed it, and make sure the equipment used in scenes isn't harming the subs.

The Covenant's security team takes care of everything else that isn't scene-related, and provides safety for all members and are essentially the bouncers. With the recent addition of the garden, and more private, themed rooms, the owners have expanded their self-imposed limit of 350 members. The fire marshal had approved them for 500 when the warehouse-turned-kink club first opened, but the cousins had intentionally kept that number down to maintain an elite status. Now with more room, they are increasing the membership to 500, still under the new maximum occupancy of 720.

Between Trident Security and The Covenant there's plenty of romance, suspense, and steamy encounters. Come meet the Sexy Six-Pack, their friends, family, and teammates.

The Sexy Six-Pack (Alpha Team) and Their Significant Others

- Ian "Boss-man" Sawyer: Devon and Nick's brother; retired Navy SEAL; co-owner of Trident Security and The Covenant; husband/Dom of Angelina (Angel).
- Devon "Devil Dog" Sawyer: Ian and Nick's brother; retired Navy SEAL; co-owner of Trident Security and The Covenant; husband/Dom of Kristen; father of John Devon "JD."
- Ben "Boomer" Michaelson: retired Navy SEAL; explosives and ordnance specialist; husband/Dom of Katerina; son of Rick and Eileen.
- Jake "Reverend" Donovan: retired Navy SEAL; sniper; husband/Dom of Nick;

brother of Mike; Whip Master at The Covenant.

- Brody "Egghead" Evans: retired Navy SEAL; computer specialist; husband/Dom of Fancy.
- Marco "Polo" DeAngelis: retired Navy SEAL; communications specialist and back up helicopter pilot; husband/Dom of Harper; father to Mara.
- Nick "Junior" Sawyer: Ian and Devon's brother; retired Navy SEAL; husband/submissive of Jake.
- Kristen "Ninja-girl" Sawyer: author of romance/suspense novels; wife/submissive of Devon; mother of "JD."
- Angelina "Angie/Angel" Sawyer: graphic artist; wife/submissive of Ian.
- Katerina "Kat" Michaelson: dog trainer for law enforcement and private agencies; wife/submissive of Boomer.
- Millicent "Harper" DeAngelis: lawyer; wife/submissive of Marco; mother of Mara.
- Francine "Fancy" Maguire: baker; wife/submissive of Brody.

Extended Family, Friends, and Associates of the Sexy Six-Pack

- Mitch Sawyer: Cousin of Ian, Devon, and Nick; co-owner/manager of The Covenant, Dom to Tyler and Tori.
- T. Carter: US spy and assassin; works for covert agency Deimos; Dom of Jordyn.
- Jordyn Alvarez: US spy and assassin; member of covert agency Deimos; submissive of Carter.
- Tyler Ellis: Stockbroker; lifestyle switch—Dom of Tori; submissive of Mitch.
- Tori Freyja: K9 trainer for veterans in need of assistance/service dogs; submissive of Mitch and Tyler.
- Parker Christiansen: owner of New Horizons Construction; husband/Dom of Shelby; adoptive father of Franco and Victor.
- Shelby Christiansen: stay-at-home mom; two-time cancer survivor; wife/submissive of Parker; adoptive mother of Franco and Victor.
- Curt Bannerman: retired Navy SEAL; owner of Halo Customs, a motorcycle repair and detail shop; husband of Dana; stepfather of Ryan, Taylor, Justin, and Amanda. Lives in Iowa.
- Dana Prichard-Bannerman: teacher; widow of retired SEAL Eric Prichard; wife

of Curt; mother of Ryan, Taylor, Justin, and Amanda. Lives in Iowa.

- Jenn "Baby-girl" Mullins: college student; goddaughter of Ian; "niece" of Devon, Brody, Jake, Boomer, and Marco; father was a Navy SEAL; parents murdered.
- Mike Donovan: owner of the Irish pub, Donovan's; brother of Jake; submissive to Charlotte.
- Charlotte "Mistress China" Roth: Parole officer; Domme and Whip Master at The Covenant; Domme of Mike.
- Travis "Tiny" Daultry: former professional football player; head of security at The Covenant and Trident compound; occasional bodyguard for TS.
- Doug "Bullseye" Henderson: retired Marine; head of the Personal Protection Division of TS.
- Rick and Eileen Michaelson: Boomer's parents; guardians of Alyssa. Rick is a retired Navy SEAL.
- Charles "Chuck" and Marie Sawyer: Ian, Devon, and Nick's parents. Charles is a self-made real estate billionaire. Marie is a plastic surgeon involved with Operation Smile.
- Will Anders: Assistant Curator of the

Tampa Museum of Art; Kristen Anders's cousin.

- Dr. Roxanne London: pediatrician; Domme/wife (Mistress Roxy) of Kayla; Whip Master at Covenant.
- Kayla London: social worker; submissive/wife of Roxanne.
- Grayson and Remington Mann: twins; owners of Black Diamond Records; Doms/fiancés of Abigail; members of The Covenant.
- Abigail Turner: personal assistant at Black Diamond Records; submissive/fiancée of Gray and Remi.
- Chase Dixon: retired Marine Raider; owner of Blackhawk Security; associate of TS.
- Reggie Helm: lawyer for TS and The Covenant; Dom/husband of Colleen.
- Alyssa Wagner: teenager saved by Jake from an abusive father; lives with Rick and Eileen Michaelson.
- Dr. Trudy Dunbar: Psychologist.
- Carl Talbot: college professor; Dom and Whip Master at The Covenant.
- Jase Atwood: Contract agent/mercenary; Lives on the island of St. Lucia; Dom of Brie.

- Brie Hanson: Owner of Daddy-O's in St. Lucia; submissive of Jase.

The Omega Team and Their Significant Others

- Cain "Shades" Foster: retired Secret Service agent.
- Tristan "Duracell" McCabe: retired Army Special Forces
- Logan "Cowboy" Reese: retired Marine Special Forces; former prisoner of war. Boyfriend/Dom of Dakota.
- Valentino "Romeo" Mancini: retired Army Special Forces; former FBI Hostage Rescue Team (HRT) member.
- Darius "Batman" Knight: retired Navy SEAL; husband/Dom of Tahira.
- Kip "Skipper" Morrison: retired Army; former LAPD SWAT sniper.
- Lindsey "Costello" Abbott: retired Marine; sniper.
- Dakota Swift: Tampa PD undercover police officer; submissive girlfriend to Logan.
- Tahira: Princess of Timasur, a small North African nation; wife/submissive of Darius.

Trident Support Staff

- Colleen McKinley-Helm: office manager of TS; wife/submissive of Reggie.
- Tempest "Babs" Van Buren: retired Air Force helicopter pilot; TS mechanic.
- Russell Adams: retired from Navy; assistant TS mechanic.
- Nathan Cook: former computer specialist with the National Security Agency (NSA).
- Conrad "CC" Chapman: retired Air Force pilot; current pilot of TS jet.
- Clinton Howe: retired Air Force pilot; TS jet co-pilot when needed.

Members of Law Enforcement

- Larry Keon: Assistant Director of the FBI.
- Frank Stonewall: Special Agent in Charge of the Tampa FBI.
- Calvin Watts: Leader of the FBI HRT in Tampa.
- Colt Parrish: Major Case Specialist, Behavioral Analysis Unit.

The K9s of Trident

- Beau: An orphaned Lab/Pit mix, rescued by Ian. Now a trained K9 who has more than earned his spot on the Alpha Team.

- Spanky: A rescued Bullmastiff with a heart of gold, owned by Parker and Shelby.
- Jagger: A rescued Rottweiler trained as an assistance/service animal for Russell.
- FUBAR: A Belgian Malinois who failed aggressive guard dog training. Adopted by Babs.
- BDSM: Bravo, Delta, Sierra, and Mike, two Belgian Malinoises and two German shepherds, the guard dogs at the Trident compound: Ian named them using the military communication's alphabet.

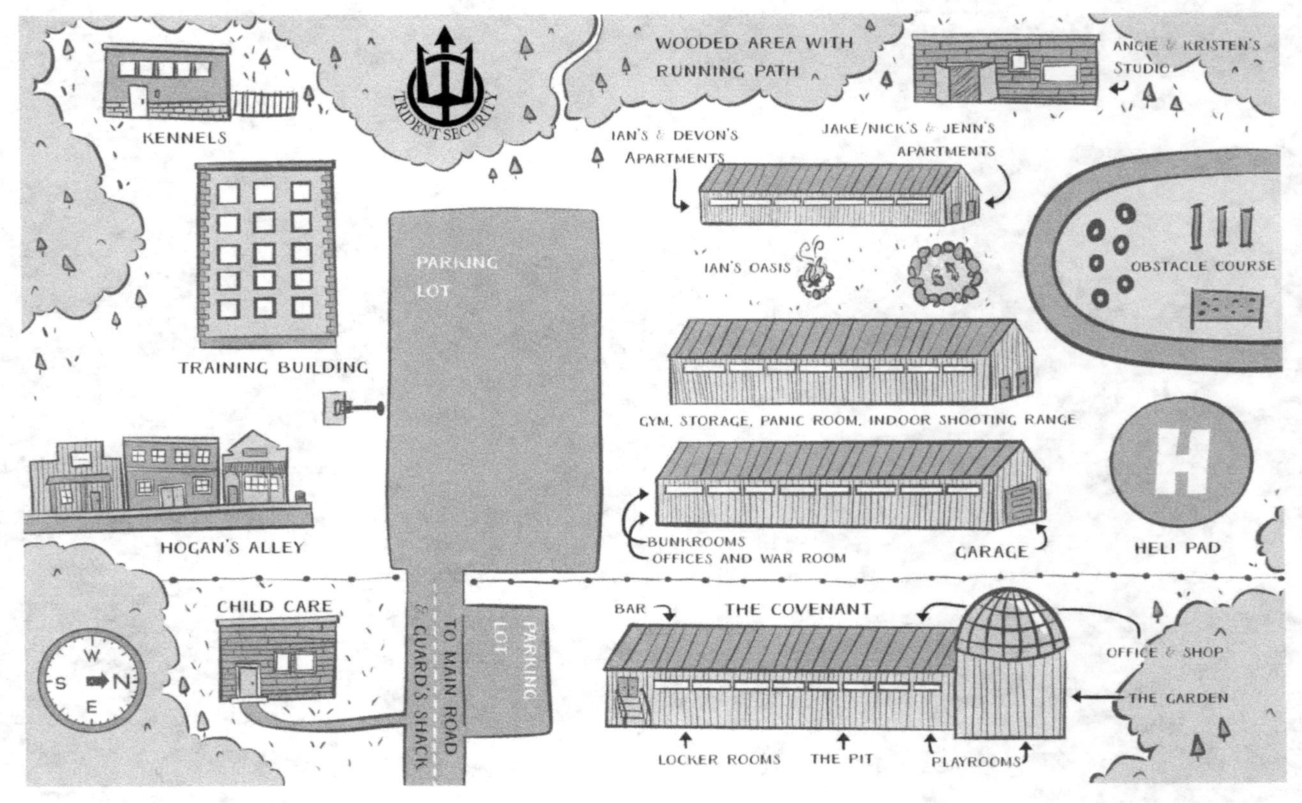

KENNELS
TRIDENT SECURITY
WOODED AREA WITH RUNNING PATH
ANGIE & KRISTEN'S STUDIO
IAN'S & DEVON'S APARTMENTS
JAKE/NICK'S & JENN'S APARTMENTS
TRAINING BUILDING
PARKING LOT
IAN'S OASIS
OBSTACLE COURSE
GYM, STORAGE, PANIC ROOM, INDOOR SHOOTING RANGE
HOGAN'S ALLEY
BUNKROOMS OFFICES AND WAR ROOM
GARAGE
HELI PAD
CHILD CARE
TO MAIN ROAD & GUARD'S SHACK
PARKING LOT
BAR
THE COVENANT
OFFICE & SHOP
THE GARDEN
LOCKER ROOMS
THE PIT
PLAYROOMS
W
N
S
E

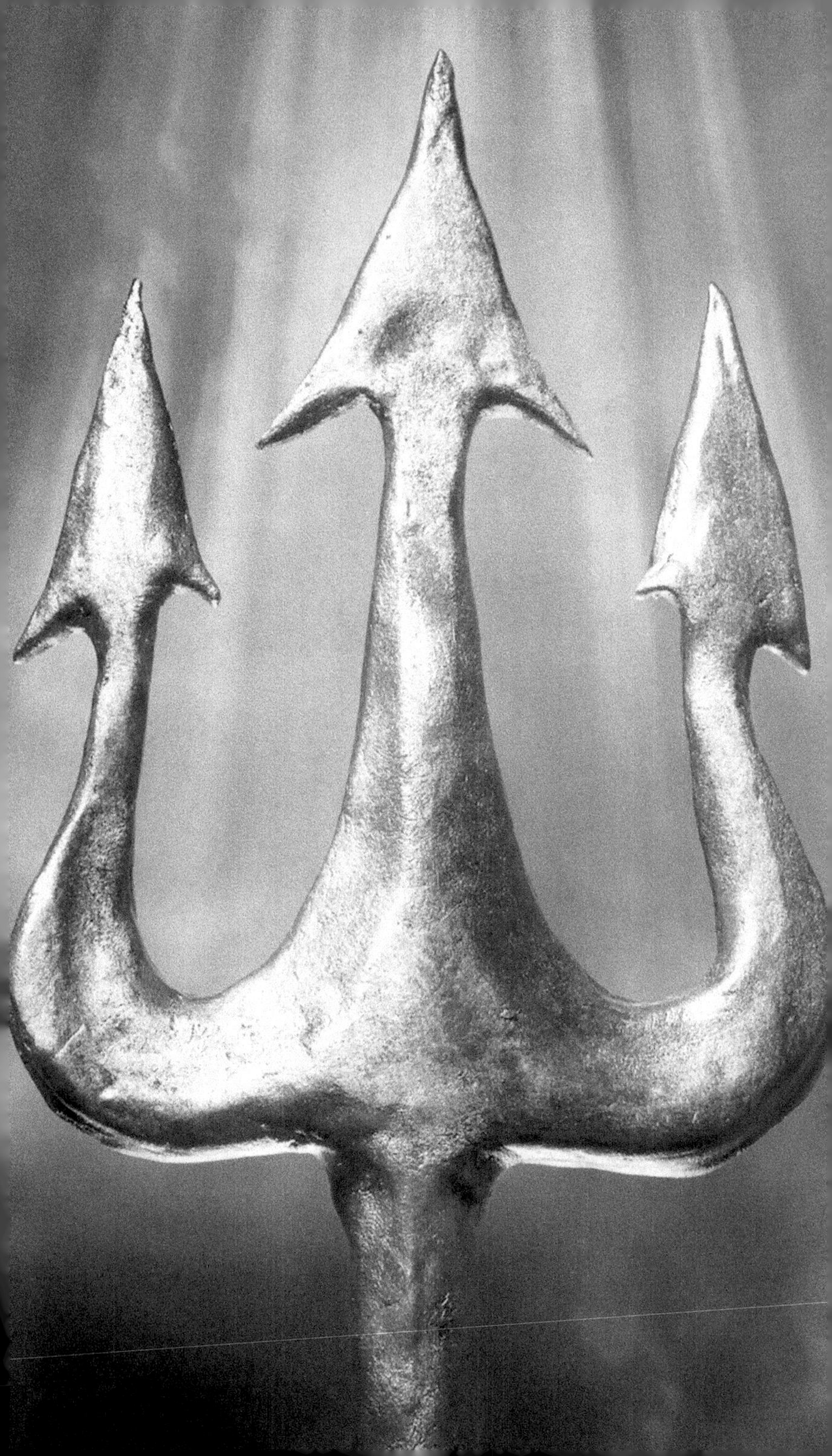

CHAPTER ONE

As the clock struck midnight in Tampa, Florida, Ian Sawyer closed the file he'd been reading, picked up the remote, and shut off the TV. CNN, Fox, MSNBC, and all the other news stations had been covering a natural gas explosion that had flattened three four-story, brownstone apartment buildings in New York City since just after 4:30 p.m. At last count, six victims had been transported to the hospital with varying degrees of injuries, while seven bodies had been pulled from the rubble. Several hours after the residential neighborhood had gone up in a fireball, NYPD, the FBI, and Homeland Security all finally confirmed there was nothing to indicate it had been an act of terrorism. In fact, 9-1-1 had received two calls about the smell of gas just minutes before the explosion. As a retired Navy SEAL and current co-owner of a private security company with numerous government contracts, Ian had a vested interest in any incident that might be terrorist-related, especially on US soil.

Standing, he stretched and smirked when his dog, Beau, did the same. The lab/pit mix had literally ended up on Ian's doorstep when he was a puppy several years ago. Ian had adopted him and trained him to be a protection dog for the fenced-in compound where he and his two brothers lived with their families. Recently they'd added four more dogs to the growing business—B.D.S.M, which stood for Bravo, Delta, Sierra, and Mike—two Belgian Malinoises and two German Shepherds. Their names had been a nod to Ian's other venture, The Covenant, a lifestyle club that he owned with his brother Devon and their cousin, Mitch, which was also located within the compound. As a result of the new canine additions, Beau's duties had been modified, and he was now in charge of protecting Ian's pregnant wife, Angie, and Devon's wife, Kristen, and son, JD.

Beau's collar had a fob on it that opened doggie doors throughout the four buildings on the property, as well as one in the fence that separated the one that housed the club from the rest of them. The dog could come and go as he pleased and got plenty of exercise during the day, which meant Ian didn't need to take him for a walk before going to bed.

Turning out the lights in the living room, he

ambled down the hallway to the master bedroom suite. The apartment was huge, just like the other three in the building, and could rival any penthouse in Tampa. After Ian had gotten over his initial shock that he was going to be a father, he'd insisted on hiring a cleaning woman to come in twice a week. At first, Angie had argued with him about it—she had her own way of doing things—but as the pregnancy progressed, and she'd gotten tired easily, she'd reluctantly agreed he'd been right. Now, she admitted to looking forward to having the woman stay on for at least the next few months. Ian was more than happy to keep the woman on indefinitely, so Angie could spend her time enjoying their new baby and getting rest whenever she needed it. He'd already moved things around in his TS office and created a baby corner, in case his wife needed a break from their newborn. A portable crib and changing table had been installed last week, to go with a small cabinet stocked with anything and everything the baby might need. His mother had laughed when he'd told her about it in their last phone conversation. Meanwhile his father had said he was glad to hear his oldest son had gotten his fair share of "smart" genes when it came to keeping the peace in his marriage. Dev had been mad he hadn't thought of all that when JD had been born, but he'd quickly rectified the situation and now had a similar set up in his own office. Notwithstanding his father's tongue-in-cheek remark,

Ian was looking forward to spending time with his child whenever he could. However, before meeting Angie, he'd thought he wouldn't be having any kids, despite the natural protective and nurturing instincts, among a few other traits, that made him a Dominant in the BDSM lifestyle.

Passing one of the two smaller bedrooms, Ian glanced inside where all the neutral-gender baby stuff was waiting for the new arrival. Gone were the pinks and purples that had been the decor after his goddaughter, Jenn Mullins, had come to live with him after her parents had been murdered. She now lived in one of the other apartments by herself, while finishing up her college education and an internship in social work. Ian and the rest of the TS Alpha team were her unofficial uncles. Having watched her grow from the moment she'd been born, the six men were having trouble coming to terms with the fact she was now a grown woman. They now had to sit back and let her make her own decisions in life, but that didn't mean they wouldn't give any guy she dated the third degree. They'd make sure the man who won Jenn's heart would know he'd be fed to the sharks in the Gulf of Mexico if he ever did anything to hurt her.

Little Bit, as Ian and Angie had dubbed their child, was due in five days, but according to the obstetrician, the baby could come at any moment during the next week or so. That announcement from yesterday's appointment had been driving Ian nuts. Modern science could predict tsunamis, find a black hole fifty-five million light years away, and create artificial limbs with a freaking 3D printer, but they couldn't tell him what day his kid was going to be born.

With Beau following, Ian entered the master bedroom. The faint moonlight peeking through the window blinds enabled him to make out his sleeping wife's form. He was glad she was out like a light, given how uncomfortable her back and legs had been lately and how often she had to get up to use the bathroom each night. How men thought women were the weaker sex was beyond Ian. He knew it wasn't true, and Angie hadn't even gone into labor yet. She'd suffered through horrible morning sickness early in her pregnancy, which had then morphed into managing day-to-day activities while having the equivalent of a medicine ball strapped to her abdomen 24/7. And now, she faced trying to push a watermelon through something tight enough to strangle his cock. Nope, women were definitely the stronger sex, and Ian was man enough to admit it.

As Beau spun a few circles on his large dog pillow on the floor in one corner of the room, Ian climbed into the king-sized bed and tried to get comfortable without waking Angie. Unfortunately, he wasn't successful.

"What time is it?" she murmured.

"Just past midnight. Go back to sleep."

"Mmm. Can't. Gotta pee." She paused, then added, "Can you go for me?"

He chuckled, but the truth was he'd do anything humanly possible for his wife, lover, and submissive, including sharing the responsibility of raising their child. Unfortunately, getting up and taking a piss for her was not something he was able to do. "Wish I could, Angel."

Throwing back the covers, she awkwardly maneuvered her body until her legs swung off the side of the bed and struggled to sit up. Ian kept his hands to himself. The last time he'd tried to help her, like a good Dom should, she'd nearly bitten his head off. Her hormones were wreaking havoc on her moods, causing them to swing wildly, and many days Ian had to tread lightly. He knew she didn't mean to snap at him and had let her get away with a few things that normally would've resulted in a punishment. Other times, it had been obvious to him his kinky wife had been subtly asking for some form of discipline, and he'd given it to her within reason. Thankfully, Angie had been using the same obstetrician Kristen had used, one that was in the lifestyle and understood the different types of play. If Dr. Sellares knew her patients practiced BDSM, she provided the couples with a list of acceptable activities that wouldn't harm the baby or mother-to-be.

As he waited for Angie to return, Ian turned onto

his side and closed his eyes. He wouldn't fall asleep until she was back in bed. Years in the Navy and being on black-ops missions had taught him how to control his sleep. He could nod off immediately if he wanted to, or rest with his eyes shut while still being aware of his surroundings.

Behind the bathroom door, the toilet flushed, and simultaneously, his cell phone chirped from where he'd placed it on his nightstand. Its low beeps were just loud enough to wake him but not Angie if they'd both been asleep. Knowing if someone was calling him at this hour it couldn't be for anything good, Ian snatched up the device and connected the call without looking at the screen. "Sawyer."

"Ian, it's Dad."

At the strange tone in his father's voice, he threw the comforter and sheet aside and sat up. Beau was at his feet before he even spoke. "What's wrong?"

"I need you on the jet to the Philippines as soon as you can. Your mom is… she's missing, Ian. Someone took her."

"Wh—"

"She—she went to town with one of the nurses to run some errands just after eight this morning. When they didn't come back in an hour like they were supposed to, we figured they were delayed and would be back soon. After another half hour, I called her cell phone, but it went to voice mail, so I grabbed one of the guides and we went looking for them. We found their vehicle about two miles up the road, pushed off the side of the road and down a hill. It was empty, but Marie's and Jocelyn's phones were left on the seats. A young boy who lives nearby said he saw three or four men block the road, and when the women stopped, they were pulled out of the SUV and forced into a van. One of the men then sent the SUV down the hill. Ian, he's not certain, but he thinks the men had guns. The boy didn't think either woman was injured, but we checked the hospital and another clinic anyway. The police took a report and are out looking for them, but there's not much to go on."

Ian had already grabbed his go-bag out of the walk-in closet as he was listening to his father rush to explain the situation, and then he pulled out a clean pair of BDUs and a T-shirt from his dresser drawers to change into. Having turned on the bedside lamp, Angie was sitting on the edge of the mattress, wide-eyed, watching him. He stopped and looked at her when his father said, "I know this is a lot to ask right now, with Angie ready to have the baby, but I need you and the teams here. We have no idea who has them, where they are, and why they were taken."

"We'll be there as soon as we can, Dad. I promise we'll find them, and then I'll be back in Tampa in time to see my kid born." He'd accept nothing less.

As he got a few more details from his father, Ian's heart was breaking. Even though she still didn't fully know what was going on yet, Angie's eyes were watery, and her lips were trembling. All she'd figured out so far was that he was leaving to go halfway around the world, where Charles and Marie Sawyer had been doing charity work, right before she was due to give birth to their first child.

Ian's mother was a plastic surgeon who donated time each year to Operation Smile, traveling to the poorer areas in Third World countries to perform reconstructive surgery on children who suffered from a variety of facial deformities. Charles, known to family and friends as Chuck, was a self-made real estate billionaire who could afford to travel with his wife and donate his time to help improve the poor areas she visited. When the four Sawyer brothers were young, they'd gone with their folks for a few weeks each summer and pitched in too.

Hanging up the phone, he kneeled in front of Angie. At some point, Beau had jumped onto the bed to comfort his distressed mistress. Since he couldn't put his head in her lap because of the baby, he was snuggled up against her hip. Ian grabbed Angie's hand. "Mom's missing, Angel. I have to go."

"Oh my God, Ian! What do you mean she's missing?"

He quickly filled her in, then continued. "I've got to get Dev, Nick, and Jake, then call the rest of the teams." Devon and Kristen lived in the apartment above them, while the youngest Sawyer brother, Nick, aka Junior, lived with his husband, Jake "Reverend"

Donovan, above Jenn's. All three men were on the TS Alpha Team. Jake had been on SEAL Team Four with Dev and Ian, while Nick had spent his SEAL tours with Team Three in San Diego before retiring less than a year ago to join his brothers and Jake in Tampa.

Grabbing her cell phone from the nightstand, Angie waved him out of the way so she could get to her feet. "I can help make the calls. I'll start with Omega Team while you take Alpha and anyone else you need to get ahold of."

Before she could hurry away, he stopped her momentum, cupped her cheeks, and stared down at her. The most amazing thing that'd ever happened to him had been the day he'd met her. The second most being the day he'd married her. He wanted the third thing to be the moment he saw her bring their child into the world. Would he miss it? God, he hoped not. But if that happened, he knew Angie wouldn't go through it alone. Kristen, Jenn, and the other women associated with Trident Security, and a few from The Covenant, would all have her six. Their extended family took care of their own, and if he couldn't be there, she'd have the best support team ever. "I'll be back in time for Little Bit, Angel."

Her gaze softened. "I know you'll try, Ian, and *I'll* try to make sure we wait, but Little Bit needs you to find Marie. She's the only grandmother our baby will have."

How the hell he'd gotten so damn lucky to have this beautiful woman fall in love with him, he'd never know, but he'd always be grateful. Bending down, he gave her a swift kiss on the lips. "I love you, Angel."

"I love you too. Now, let's get busy."

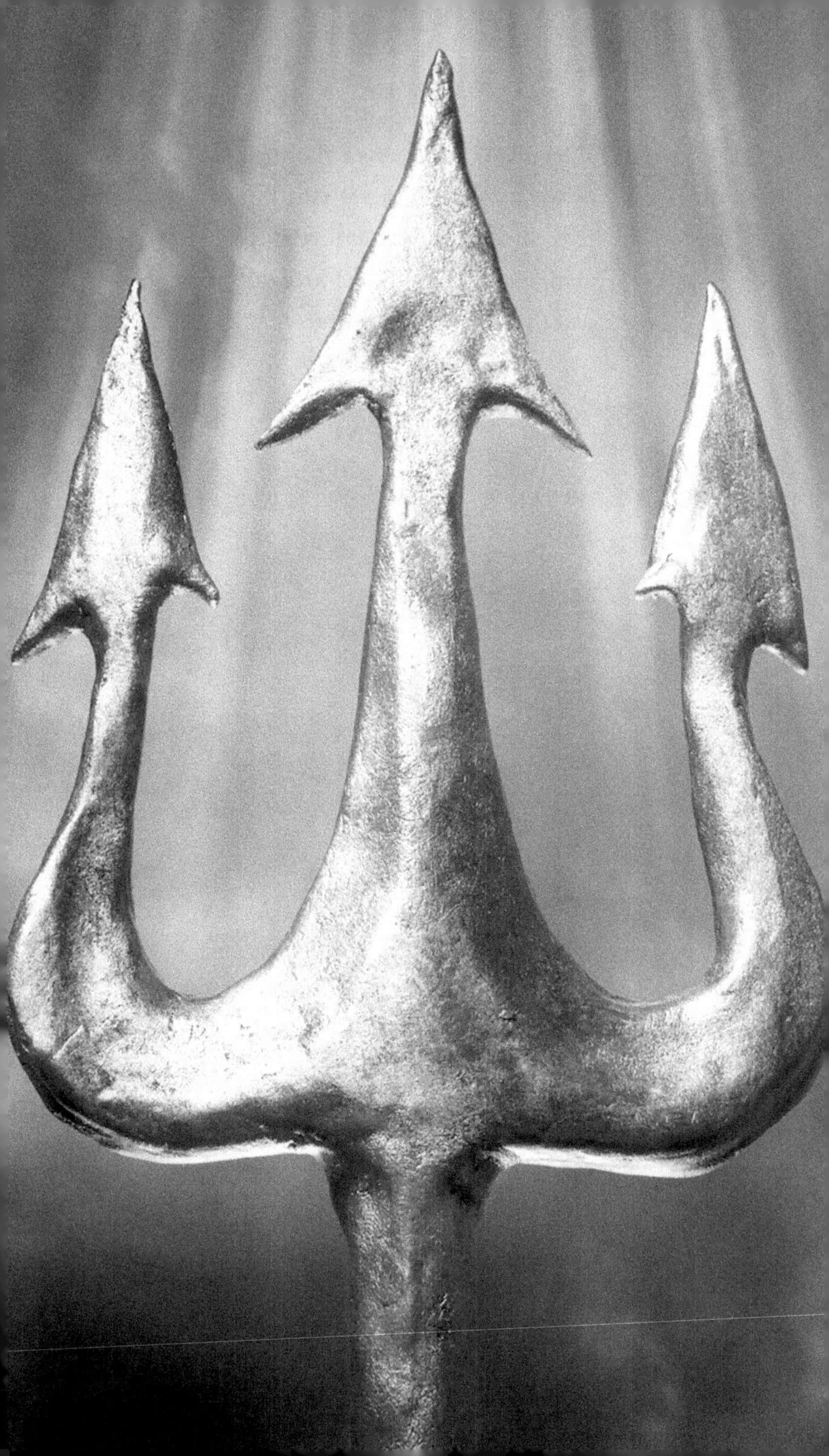

CHAPTER TWO

Somewhere in the province of Davao del
Norte, Philippines…

As Marie Sawyer heard the door unlock, her heart pounded in her chest. The cool air coming through a ceiling vent had been giving her goosebumps for the past hour or so. Central air conditioning in the Philippines was a luxury only the rich could afford. She still didn't know where she and Jocelyn Navarro were or why they'd been abducted in the first place. Their wrists had been tied, and their heads covered with potato sacks just moments after they'd been forced at gunpoint into the van that'd blocked the road they'd been traveling on. The only thing they'd seen since was the inside of the bedroom they'd been shoved into after the heavy twine used to bind their wrists had been cut away. By the time she'd ripped the sack off her head, the door had been slammed shut and locked.

The room had a queen-sized bed, which they were sitting on, some sparse furniture, and nothing more. The attached bath had even less. The windows in both had been blacked out by a tarp that hung outside. An overhead lamp was their only light. It hadn't taken long to realize there was no way out and nothing available to use as a weapon. Marie was certain her sons would argue with her about that. As trained Navy SEALs, they could probably find an exit and take down a bunch of the bad guys without blinking an eye. At seventy-one, she doubted she could overtake any of the younger, larger men holding them hostage. She might be able to outsmart them, but a physical fight was out of the question with no weapons at hand.

Aside from a few English commands, their captors had spoken Cebuano, one of the several local languages. Jocelyn was from the Philippines but had gotten an education in the United States where her father had been an ambassador. She understood what they'd been saying, for all the good it had done. The four men hadn't revealed anything in either language to help the two women figure out why they were there —wherever *there* was.

Although they'd been forced to leave their cell and satellite phones behind, Marie still had her multi-function watch Ian had given her for Christmas a few years ago. It was a very durable, sleek, military-style design, and she didn't have to worry about losing or damaging the gold one she usually wore while visiting a lesser-developed country where her charity work often took her. By her calculations, they'd traveled on a mix of paved and unpaved roads for fifty minutes or so. She and Jocelyn had left to run errands two municipalities over from where they'd been staying. They'd wanted to refill the clinic's tiny stock room with supplies that didn't necessarily have anything to do with medicine, such as feminine pads, baby formula, cloth diapers, shampoo, soap, canned goods, and batteries, among other things. The medical supplies and drugs were covered by the non-profit charity. Chuck and Marie were supposed to head back to the States tomorrow. Instead of going straight home to Charlotte, North Carolina, they were planning a detour to Tampa to await the arrival of their second grandchild.

God, please let me live to see Angie and Ian's baby. Don't let this beautiful time in their lives be marred by my death.

Jocelyn and Marie quickly got to their feet as the door swung open, and a tall, intimidating man stepped inside. Out in the hallway, two men armed with assault rifles stood sentry. The one who'd entered the room gestured toward the door. "Let's go."

Grabbing Jocelyn's arm to prevent her from obeying the barked order, Marie stood her ground. "Where? Who are you and why are we here?"

The man sneered at her. "Who I am is not important. As for the rest, come with me and find out."

Marie lifted her chin at the challenge in his voice, then glanced at the pistol holstered at his hip. Her mind raced, but there weren't any options. Whatever was going on, they weren't going to learn about it in the empty room.

Hooking her arm around Jocelyn's, she stepped forward. When the man was convinced they'd follow, he led the way out the door.

Well, they were in a house—a very large one by Philippine standards. Expensive art hung on the walls, while fine china and crystal stood on tabletops and in wall niches as they walked down a hallway to a flight of marble-covered stairs, undoubtedly the one they'd climbed earlier. As the man descended the staircase, Marie glanced over her shoulder. The two armed lackeys were right behind them, so they had no choice but to keep moving along.

They trailed behind their escort, across the massive foyer and into an equally impressive living room. It was finely decorated with the "expensive" theme she'd seen throughout the rest of the house, so far, except for the bedroom they'd just left.

"Welcome, Dr. Sawyer, or may I call you Marie?" The husky voice belonged to a stocky man who was sitting in a wingback chair. "Please, have a seat." He gestured toward two couches while puffing away on a cigar.

Marie stared at the middle-aged man. She didn't recognize him but was surprised he knew who she was. That fact didn't make her feel any better. "I'd rather stand while you tell me who you are, why my friend and I were kidnapped, and how you know my name."

He snorted, then took a sip of what looked like brandy from a snifter. "Kidnapped? Such an inappropriate word in this case, isn't it? Clearly, neither of you are children as the word implies. Let's just say you're here on a job interview, and I research all my prospective employees. Sit, and I'll explain."

When she refused to comply with his order, his eyes narrowed, and his expression grew hard. "I will not ask you again, Dr. Sawyer. While you are invaluable to me, your nurse is not." Marie heard a gasp and turned to see the man who'd brought them there had one hand wrapped around Jocelyn's upper arm and the other pointing his gun to her head. The younger woman's tear-filled eyes were wide, and her face had paled significantly, while her entire body shook. Meanwhile, their unidentified host continued. "Nurses are much easier to come by than a woman of your caliber. If you insist on being uncooperative, she will pay for it."

Marie had no choice. Stepping over to one of the couches, she sat, perched on the edge of the cushion. Jocelyn was shoved in her direction and then sat next to her, sobbing softly. Marie grasped her hand and squeezed before glaring at the man seated across from them. "Fine. We're sitting. You said you'd explain—I'm waiting. And am I supposed to call you, 'hey, you,' or do you have a name?"

Yes, she probably sounded like she had when her boys had been younger and had gotten in trouble for one reason or another, but she refused to show how frightened she was. Calmness in the face of adversity was a trait most surgeons and emergency room physicians acquired over the years. If they freaked out, their staff would follow suit, and then all hell would break loose, putting their patients in danger. While she was unnerved on the inside, all she would show was her defiance.

An amused expression crossed the man's face. "Brave woman," he said. "You don't recognize me?"

"Should I? I'm an American who has only been here for three weeks to work in a clinic, performing surgery. If you don't work at the clinic or weren't one of my patients and their families, then I wouldn't have a clue who you are."

He nodded. "Fair enough. You can call me Mr. Albano."

It was highly unlikely that was his real name—it was a very common one in that region—considering he'd abducted them. Marie had a few other choice names for him, but it was probably wise not to mention them.

"Well, Mr. Albano, I'm scheduled to return to the

States tomorrow." She took a chance, nodded toward the woman beside her, and lied. "So is Jocelyn." Actually, the nurse would be heading to a clinic on one of the other islands, joining the next Operation Smile surgeon who was arriving in a few days, but Marie was keeping that to herself. Hopefully, Jocelyn would play along. "We'll be missed, if we're not already, when we don't contact our charity to give them our final reports this evening." At least that part was true. She did have to check in with the director who handled everyone's trips and schedules.

"I'm afraid you'll be missing your flight. You see, you'll be performing surgery tomorrow."

Her brow furrowed. "Excuse me? On whom?"

The man shrugged. "A friend of mine needs to have his face reconstructed. Currently, he's too recognizable by certain, shall I say, agencies, and he'd like to change that."

Having three retired Navy SEALs for sons, whose special-ops careers had followed them into the private sector, she was far from naïve or stupid when it came to the underbelly of society. "You want me to alter some criminal's face so he can avoid being captured and prosecuted? Is that it?"

"Yes."

"You said this was a job interview. What happens if I refuse to be employed by you?"

His head tilted to the side, and he took a puff of his cigar and then blew the smoke into the air. "Then

I'm afraid I'll have no use for you or the pretty lady next to you, and no one will ever learn where you both disappeared to."

So, in other words, do the surgery or they were both dead. *Well, shit.*

She glanced at Jocelyn, before returning her attention to "Mr. Albano." In another time or place, she might have considered him to be a handsome man, but the smugness that hadn't left his face in the past few minutes radiated the evil within him, and it made him downright ugly. "Where am I supposed to perform this surgery? I need equipment, a sterile room, an anesthetist—"

"All that will be provided. A fully-stocked operating room is ready to handle all your needs, along with a small surgical staff. This is not the first time I've arranged this procedure for one of my associates. However, the plastic surgeon who'd agreed to perform the surgeries in exchange for canceling his gambling debts decided to get greedy and tried to blackmail me. Needless to say, he's no longer able to perform surgery. After his hands were removed from his body, he was released into the woods for my men to hunt. I understand he screamed like a girl before they took his head."

Marie and Jocelyn gasped at the horrible image and the nonchalance of the man who'd created it with a few simple words. This was just getting worse and worse, and Marie hated to ask her next question, but she needed to hear the answer. "What happens to us after the surgery? We'll have seen your 'associate,' as you call him, so we'll be able to identify him. You won't just let us walk out of here if we can identify you *and* him."

Albano nodded. "You'll see his face right before the surgery, at which time you'll map out the reconstruction. After the surgery, he'll be swollen and bandaged. You won't be seeing the final results at all. As long as you don't give me any problems, I'll have you both returned to San Isidro in one piece. As for being able to identify me, just by description alone, I'm not worried. One, I have plenty of local and national law enforcement in my pocket, along with several politicians. You'd never come close to having me arrested. And, two, if you try, I'll have everyone who works in and visits your clinic beheaded. Of course, I won't do it right away—I'll wait until no one sees it coming. You'll have all those deaths on your hands, Dr. Sawyer, and I doubt you want that."

"How can we trust you'll keep your word? There's nothing stopping you from killing us both when it's all over."

He frowned at her. "I'll keep my word, Dr. Sawyer, as long as you don't give me a reason not to. Now, Antonio will return you to your room, and I'll have some food prepared for you. Then I suggest you relax and get a good night's sleep. You'll want to be at your best tomorrow. Both your lives depend on it."

Antonio, the tall man who'd led them downstairs, gestured toward the doorway. "Let's go."

Standing, Marie didn't let go of Jocelyn's hand. The younger woman was barely holding it together. As they followed their escort back upstairs, Marie wondered how long it had taken her husband to contact their sons to say she was missing. Knowing Chuck, it hadn't been long. That meant Ian, Devon, Nick, her son-in-law Jake, and the rest of the Trident Security teams would be on their way to the Philippines. Glancing at her watch, she calculated the time. She just had to do everything she could to keep herself and Jocelyn alive until they got onto the island. Her boys would find them—she just hoped they wouldn't be too late.

CHAPTER THREE

Angie was trying to be brave, but it was so hard. Ian had cut back his workload a few days ago to ensure he wouldn't be far from her when she went into labor. Now he was going to be halfway around the world, and there was no way she could ask him not to go. Marie and Chuck Sawyer were the closest thing she'd had to parents these past few years. She'd been born to her own mother and father when they'd been older and not expecting any more children. Angie's brother, Sam, had been nine years older than her and had been killed in a car accident with several friends his senior year in high school. Her parents had then both died eighteen months apart in their late fifties of natural causes—at least that's what their death certificates said. Angie believed they'd both died of broken hearts, never fully recovering from the loss of their only son.

When Angie first met her future in-laws on a trip she'd taken with Ian, the older couple had been in the Philippines then too. Marie and Chuck had welcomed her to the family with open arms. Although Angie and Ian hadn't been engaged at the time, Marie had told her that even though her eldest son was gun-shy about marriage after a bad breakup with his former fiancée years before, she was certain he would come around. Angie hadn't been too sure, but the woman had been right. Seven days later, less than two hours after they'd landed at Tampa's International Airport, Ian had proposed to her. She still wasn't certain which one of them had been more shocked. It'd seemed like he'd experienced an epiphany at the time and blurted it out. But then he'd gotten all romantic and she knew the proposal had been real and honest. Not once since had she ever regretted becoming Mrs. Ian Sawyer. Her Dom and husband owned her heart, body, and soul, and she wouldn't want it any other way.

Sitting in the conference room in the Trident Security offices, with her swollen feet up on another chair, Angie wished there was something more she could do to help, other than the few phone calls she'd made. Ian was in the war-room with Brody "Egghead" Evans, Ben "Boomer" Michaelson, and Nathan "Cookie" Cook doing whatever they needed to do before heading to the local private airport where the TS jet was stored. Their pilot, CC Chapman, and occasional co-pilot, Clinton Howe, were already on their way there and would have everything ready in time to go wheels up. Since it was such a long flight, they needed the two onboard, as per regulations, so one could rest while the other flew the jet or monitored the autopilot.

Dev was in his office on the phone with Chase Dixon at Blackhawk Security, giving him the details of cases that couldn't be put on hold. BHS and Trident often backed each other up and shared resources when needed. Marco "Polo" DeAngelis, Nick, Jake, and the Omega team operatives were over in the next building gathering all the equipment, weapons, and ammo they might need. Since they had no idea what the mission would call for, they were preparing for the worst and praying for the best. With the hidden storage compartments on the jet, they'd be able to sneak their weapons into the Philippines.

Meanwhile, Kristen and Kat, Boomer's wife, were in the office break room with Jenn, filling up two coolers with sandwiches, drinks, and snacks for the two teams to fuel up on during the trans-Pacific flight to the Philippines. When Angie had called the Omega Team members, she'd asked Logan "Cowboy" Reese, who lived closest to the compound, to swing by a Publix that was open twenty-four hours a day for some rolls and lunchmeat. Between everything he'd brought, Kristen's and Angie's refrigerators, and the company's stock room, they'd be able to pack up enough food for everyone for the long trip.

The only member of either team that wasn't there was Darius "Batman" Knight who was on his honeymoon in Tahiti. After everything he and his new bride, Princess Tahira of Timasur, had gone through to get to the altar, Ian refused to call and ask Darius to cut his vacation short and meet them in the Philippines. Knowing Darius, he would've dropped everything and done just that. Instead, Ian was calling a few contacts who might be able to get boots on the ground in the province of Davao del Norte quickly and start gathering intel so it was available when the Trident jet landed. Every second counted at times like this.

Whenever they traveled, Chuck and Marie made certain their sons had their full itinerary, in case anything happened. According to the latest one they'd sent, the couple was in San Isidro, a fifth-class municipality, in other words, one of the poorer areas in Davao del Norte. Tomorrow was supposed to be the last day of their twenty-day trip before flying back to the States. Marie had apparently done several reconstructive surgeries on children with birth defects or devastating injuries, whose parents could barely put food on the table, much less pay for medical care.

Everyone was busy doing something except for Angie, Beau, who was at her feet, and JD, who was sound asleep in the portable crib they'd moved into the conference room from Devon's office, so she could watch him. Aware of the fact she wouldn't be able to do much hadn't stopped her from waddling over to the office with Kristen earlier. Her back and feet hurt, and Little Bit was kicking up a storm, but she wasn't about to tell Ian or anyone else that. They had plenty to do and worry about, and she didn't want to add to the long list.

"Hey, Ang," Marco said as he strode in with two boxes and sat down next to her. "Can you do me a favor and check these comm units with me really quick? We used them all in yesterday's training session with TPD and Blackhawk, and I need to swap out the batteries for fresh ones and make sure they're all working properly."

Surprised but happy to have something else to do than just sit there, she reached for the closest box and opened it. After replacing three or four batteries, she realized Marco hadn't needed her help. He could have done this on the eighteen- to nineteen-hour flight, including one stopover for refueling. The reason he'd asked her was to give her something to take her mind off the fact her mother-in-law was missing. Like her husband, Marco had been a Dom in the lifestyle for a long time. Taking care of a submissive's needs, mentally, emotionally, or physically, was second nature to them. It didn't matter if a sub was unattached or collared by someone else—most Doms took their roles seriously and cared for all of them.

"Thank you, Marco."

He shrugged his shoulders as he continued to

make sure the tiny earpieces were receiving and the attached microphones were transmitting. "No problem. We'll be ready to hit the road in about ten minutes, so try to get some sleep after we leave. There's no point staying awake the rest of the night when we'll just be in the air. Harper said to text her in the morning, and she'll head over with Mara."

"I will. Fancy texted me and asked if she should take the day off. I basically told her what you just told me. There's no point, since you won't be landing until late afternoon our time." Brody's wife, Fancy, owned a bakery, and she was usually there by 6:00 a.m. and would open an hour later. She also had a wonderful staff who could fill in for her at any time, which would come in handy when she had her own baby in a few months. "Logan said Dakota was working early too, but she would check in with us when she could." Cowboy's fiancée was an undercover police officer with the Tampa PD.

When she'd first agreed to marry Ian, Angie hadn't realized how close she would become to the men and women of Trident Security. At the time, Devon had been the only married teammate. But as each of the "Sexy Six-Pack," as Kristen had dubbed them, had fallen for their soulmates, and another team and other employees had been added to the mix, they'd become an extended family. As with every family, they had their ups and downs, but when one of them needed help, there was never any question of loyalty or sacrifice. Every single one of them would drop everything to support the others, no matter what needed to be done. And Angie knew they would do everything they could to find Marie and make sure Ian got back in time to see her give birth to their first child. She'd just have to pray it was enough.

———

Pacing back and forth in the war-room, Ian impatiently waited for the international call to Scotland to go through. They needed to get to the airport soon, but the teams were still loading up all the equipment and weapons while CC was with the jet doing his pre-flight checklist. Everyone knew what they were supposed to be doing—it was a tremendous help to have employees who worked together like a well-oiled machine. Ian trusted them to do their jobs and not to leave anything to chance.

"Come on, come on," he murmured as he pivoted to head back in the other direction. "Pick up the fucking—"

"Hello, Tampa!" The friendly American voice came over the room's speakers so Ian, Brody, Nathan, and Boomer could all hear it. Meanwhile, its owner's face appeared on a screen on the wall. It didn't surprise Ian that the man was wide awake and at his computer console at 5:45 a.m. BST—British Summer

Time. "It's the middle of the night over there. What can I do you for?"

"Jones, I need Mic on the line on the double," Ian barked. There was no time for pleasantries or explanations, nor were they necessary.

"On it." Samuel Jones disappeared from the screen as he ran to gather up the Steel Corps team and its leader, Bea "Mic" Michaels, one of the most kickass women Ian had ever met in his life. The original TS Alpha Team went way back with Mic since they'd all been in Iraq together—the men on SEAL Team Four and Mic with Army Intelligence. After seeing her in action, interrogating a terrorist while using forms of torture, Ian had never wanted to be on the other side of her in battle. However, she'd softened some since becoming a mother to an adorable baby girl.

Less than two minutes later, the rest of the Steel Corps team rushed in behind Jones, all having obviously been roused from their beds—Chris Jordon, Matthew "Rook" Riley, Ed Pierce, Jerimiah Flynn, Mary "Red" Bickle, and finally, Mic. Jones held out his chair for her to take, and her concerned face filled most of the screen. "What's wrong, Sawyer?"

"I know you're all packing to return to the States, but I need boots on the ground in the Philippines ASAP. My parents are on one of their charity trips, and from the sound of it, Mom and another woman were abducted not far from the clinic they were working in."

"Shit. Details?" That was Mic—short and to the point.

"Very few, which is why I need your help. A lot of shit can happen in the eighteen or so hours it's going to take us to get there." Wasn't that the truth? Right then, Ian would give anything to have teleportation be a real thing. Since it wasn't, he'd have to rely on people who could get to the Philippines much faster than the Trident teams.

She glanced over her shoulder at her team, and without hesitation, every single one of them volunteered to go. Ian had expected nothing less, and he knew Mic had too.

Turning back, she said, "Chris, Rook, Pierce, Red, and Flynn can be wheels up in thirty. Jones and I can gather intel from here. Call us from the jet and give us what you've got." She paused. "I wish I could go and be there for you too."

Ian's expression softened. "I know you do. Give PJ a kiss for me. Tell her she'll have a new cousin soon."

"Holy shit! I forgot Angie's due in a few days."

"Yup. Life loves to throw fucking curveballs, doesn't it?" Without waiting for a response, he added, "Jones, I'll call you from the jet. In the meantime, connect with Cookie over whatever secure link you two use so we can have a three-way conversation later." Nathan Cook was a former NSA computer hacker Trident had hired a while back. It had been a great deal for the company since it gave them access to the National Security Agency's database. "Mic… thanks. I owe you."

"Bullshit." She pressed a button, and the screen went dark.

Dev stuck his head into the room. "We're ready."

As Brody gathered up the two laptops and their accessories that he was bringing with him to work on, Ian and Boomer strode out of the room. They followed Devon into the conference room where the women had gathered. After kissing Jenn on the forehead, and promising he'd bring the woman she considered to be her grandmother home, safe and sound, he wrapped his arms around Angie as far as he could with her baby belly between them. He lowered his mouth to hers. When he ended the kiss, there were tears rolling down her cheeks. "Oh, Angel. You're killing me here."

Swallowing hard, she shook her head and wiped the wetness from her face. "I-I'm sorry. I wasn't going to cry, but these damn hormones—"

"Shh. I'll be back in time. Somehow, I'll make it."

Whether she believed him or not, she nodded. "We'll be waiting for you."

He kissed her one more time, as Boomer and Devon did the same to their wives, and then the three men hightailed it out to the parking lot and loaded into the idling vehicles filled with their teammates and equipment. As the caravan headed for the compound's gate, Ian's gaze remained on Angie, where she stood just outside the door to the offices with Kristen, Jenn, and Kat until she was out of sight. Sending up a silent prayer, he asked God, and any other powers that might exist, to get him home in time, with his parents and the teams in tow, in time to see Little Bit enter the world, kicking and screaming.

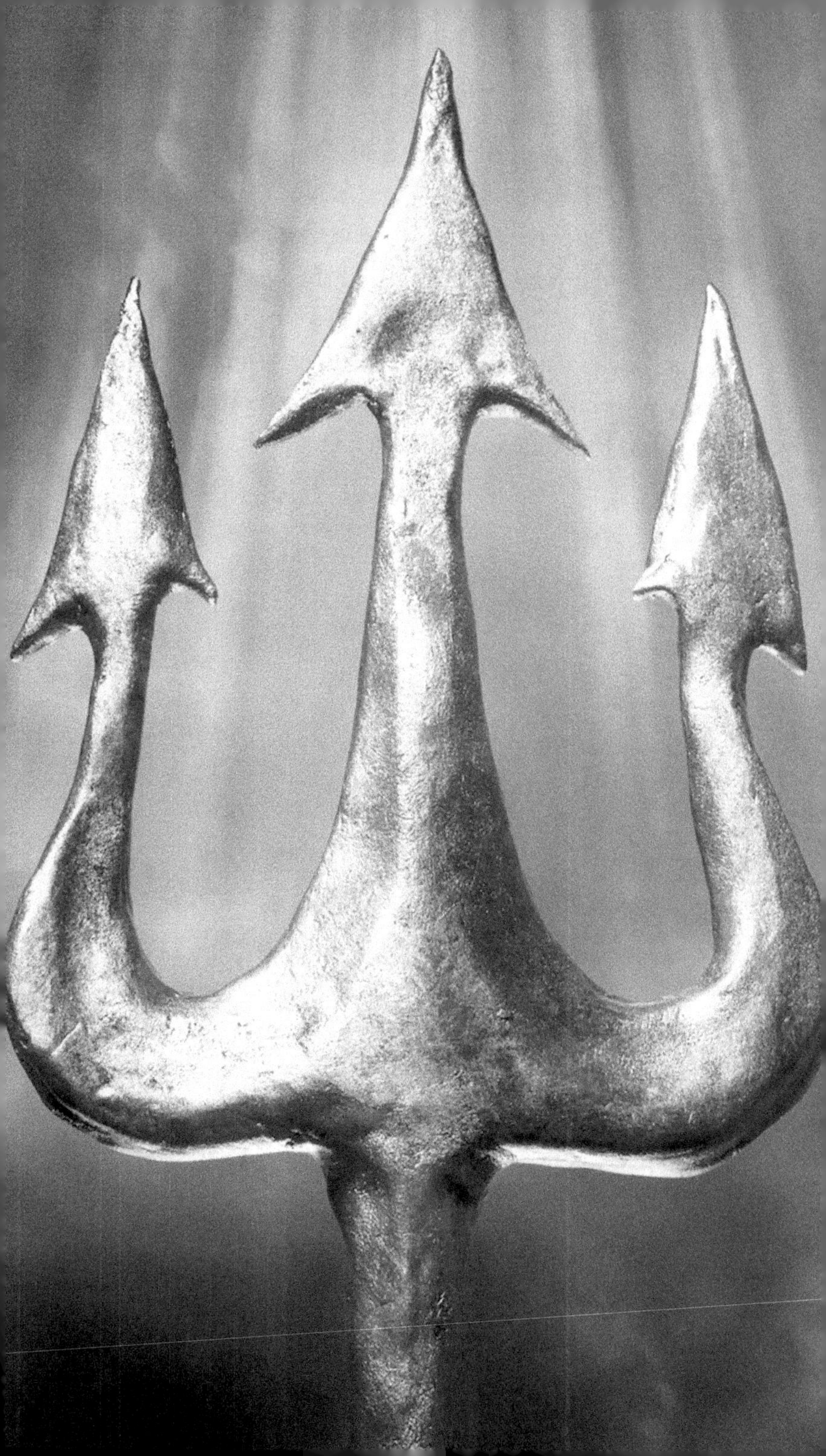

CHAPTER FOUR

After making certain JD was all set in his baby swing, Kristen sat at her computer desk in the studio that housed her and Angie's workspaces. It'd been her sister-in-law's idea to have the structure built on the compound's property, so they had a place where they could both be comfortable to work and hang out together, instead of in either one's apartment. The large, 800-square-foot, well-lit room had been broken up into five areas. In addition to Kristen's desk, where she could write and edit her books, there was another section where Angie could explore her various artistic talents, a small kitchen, and a sitting area. Finally, there was a play area for JD, the soon-to-arrive Little Bit, and any visiting little ones. They'd also installed a full bath in case any kids ever got too messy.

It was a little after 10:00 a.m., still hours before

the TS jet would land in the Philippines, so the women and their friends were trying to get some work done—as hard as it was—to take their minds off Marie. Angie was designing a new romance novel cover for Kristen's publisher, Red Rose Books. Marco's wife, Harper, a lawyer, was curled up on the couch, preparing a court brief, while her toddler, Mara, played with some colorful blocks nearby. Kat was outside with fellow K9 trainer Tori Frejya, who was engaged to Mitch Sawyer and his ménage partner Tyler Ellis. They were putting Bravo and Delta through tactical obedience exercises with their K9 handlers, operatives from the new Personal Protection Division at Trident. Fancy should be arriving soon— she'd stayed at the bakery through the morning rush. And, last but not least, Shelby Christiansen was sitting in a recliner, beta reading for an indie author Kristen had introduced her to. She'd been a reader for Kristen for several years now, even before they'd ever met in person. While Shelby was there supporting her friends, the petite woman's two adopted sons, Franco and Victor, were with her husband, Parker, a construction company owner, touring his work sites for a few hours and probably loving every minute.

The only other person not there besides Logan's fiancée, Dakota Swift, who knew what was going on and they trusted not to leak the information anywhere, was Kristen's cousin Will Anders. The only reason he wasn't there was that the museum where he worked received a new exhibit that morning, and he needed to catalog over two hundred artifacts and compare the list to the manifest. It was an all-day job, but he checked in every hour or so.

After going through her latest emails, Kristen signed into Facebook to check her notifications and private messages. She started with the latter and responded to several of them before she got to the one from a reader named Rhonda, who was a big fan and very active in the Kristen Anders' Amazing Angels reader group.

Hi Kristen! Sorry to be the bearer of bad news, but I came across a book by a new "author," and I hate to say it, but it looks like she plagiarized your *Hearts Ablaze*. You might want to take a look at it. The names have been changed but almost everything else is word for word! She has three other books out, all rapidly released. I checked the sample chapters of the other two. One sounds really familiar, and I'm trying to remember which author might have written it. The other isn't one of yours either. Sorry!

"Shit," she murmured, clicking on the link that'd been provided. Of course, it would be one of her indie books instead of the others she had with her traditional publisher. Red Rose Books had a large legal department that handled stuff like this, but if *Hearts Ablaze* had, indeed, been plagiarized, Kristen would need to retain her own lawyer.

Once she was on the book's purchase page, she read the blurb. It wasn't exactly the same as the one Kristen had written for *Hearts Ablaze*, but it was close enough. Her stomach was already tied up in knots thinking about Marie and what Chuck and their sons must be going through, and this wasn't helping. Bringing up the sample, and praying Rhonda had been wrong, Kristen started to read.

"Son of a freakin' witch!" She'd gotten creative in her cursing since JD had been born and Mara had started repeating everything she heard. Ian was still in trouble with Harper because her daughter was very fond of the word "twatwaffle." Thankfully, it sounded more like "what-waffle" coming from the little girl's mouth.

"What's the matter?" Shelby asked from across the room.

Gaping at the screen, Kristen couldn't answer right away, too shocked by what she was reading. Rhonda had been right. All this so-called author had done was replace the main characters' names, Keith and Shannon, with Kevin and Sharon. She hadn't even been original about it! The fictional town had also been changed from Pine Creek to Aspen Creek.

"What's wrong, Kristen?"

Shelby now stood directly behind her, and Kristen gestured to the screen. "She… she stole my book! I've been plagiarized! I can't believe this! Let me bring up *Hearts Ablaze*." Opening another browser window, she went back to the same site and located the first book she'd ever published—the one that'd propelled her into the indie author world before she'd been discovered by Red Rose. She clicked on the sample and lined up the two windows side by side. "Look. Word for freaking word except the names, and even those are similar."

It didn't take long for Shelby to blurt out, "Oh, my God! I don't believe it! Who is this person?"

"January Moore—although I doubt that's her real name." Fury overtook her shock as she clicked on the thief's name to go to the author page for more information. "I've never heard of her, and look, she only has three books, and they were all published in the past ten days. Yeah, some legit authors do rapid releases all the time, but it's also common with book thieves. Rhonda from my reader group was the one who noticed it. She looked at these other two and said they weren't mine, but she thought she read one of them before and is trying to figure out what book it might've been.

"You know, every time someone posted about being plagiarized in the author groups I'm in, I was so happy it wasn't me. Now, I know how they felt—like my heart has been ripped from my chest. And it's not even one of my books with Red Rose, so I have to hire a lawyer if the site won't take them down."

"Um, free lawyer standing right behind you, sweetie," Harper said.

Kristen glanced over her shoulder to see Harper and Angie, who had joined them and were studying the split screen on the computer monitor. "Lawyer, yes. Free, no. I won't let you work for nothing, Harper—it's not like I can't afford it—but I'll hire you if I need to."

It wouldn't be the first time the woman had been Kristen's legal counsel. She'd been a tremendous help when Kristen's first husband had tried to claim he was entitled to half the royalties from her "little books," as he'd called them, despite their divorce. The case had been dropped after Tom had been arrested for embezzling money from his brokerage firm. Kristen still had a hard time wrapping her brain around the fact a man she'd loved and married was now in federal prison, serving a four-year sentence.

"Let me… shoot, let me download her book, so I have the proof before I email the site to try to get it taken down. I don't know what to do after that. Do I sue her for the money she earned from sales of the book? Is it worth the time and effort to do that? I mean, it's only been up a few days—they wait sixty days before paying out royalties, so she'll never see the money if they take the book down. I-I… damn it.

How could someone do this? I mean, I put my blood, sweat, and tears into—" Her voice caught in her throat, and tears rolled down her cheeks. Of all days, she did not need this happening today.

Shelby squeezed her shoulders. "Don't worry. Between us, we'll take this bee-otch down. I'll download the other two books and get online with Rhonda to try to figure out who they were stolen from. If she stole yours, most likely, she stole the others too. Those authors need to be told, whoever they are."

If that was the case, Kirsten wasn't looking forward to letting the other authors know they'd been plagiarized too. However, in the indie community, authors, readers, and everyone else watched out for each other for the most part. "Damn it!"

"Bam it! Bam it, An-ten."

Kristen hadn't realized Mara had wandered over to them. "An-ten" was baby speak for Aunt Kristen. She rolled her eyes and glanced at Harper. "Sorry."

The other woman shrugged and waved her hand. "It's not as bad as what Uncle Ian says. Don't worry about it—I'm loose-lipped, too, when I'm in a bad mood. I've just been able to get away with it so far."

"Bam it! Bam it! Bam it!"

Great, just what they needed today.

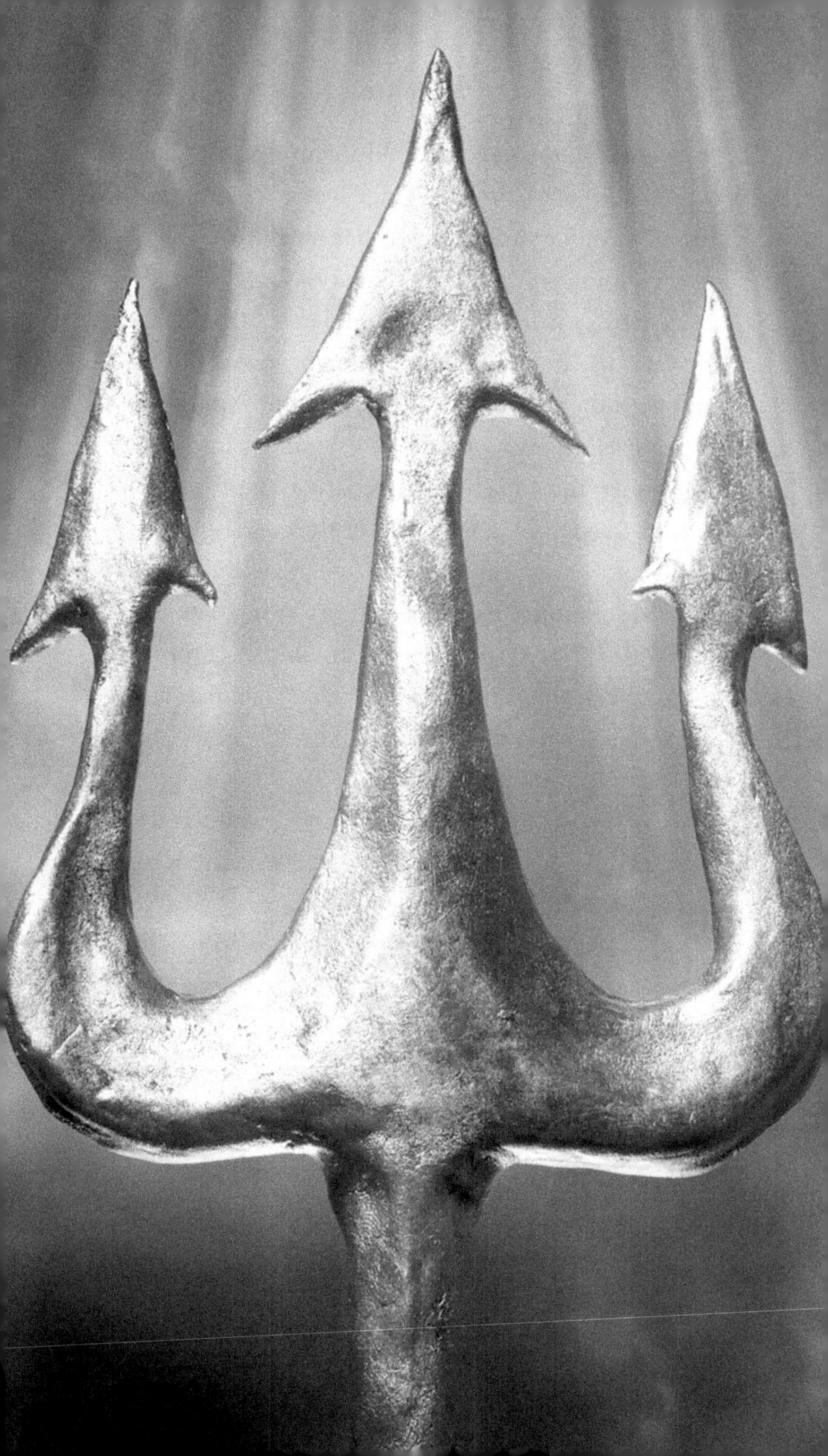

CHAPTER FIVE

As Nick stood from his front-row seat next to him, Jake opened his eyes. Like almost everyone else aboard the jet, they'd been trying to get some sleep, even though worry had made it difficult to shut down their minds. While, over the years, they'd all trained themselves to take advantage of downtime in order to revitalize their bodies, despite everything going on around them, it was difficult to do when the mission was personal. Marie might not have given birth to all the operatives currently flying over the Pacific Ocean on their way to rescue her, but she was a mother to them all the same. Hell, if it hadn't been for Marie kicking Jake's ass, figuratively, he might've lost the best thing that'd ever happened to him—her youngest son, Nick.

"Where are you going?" Jake asked in a low voice so as to not wake anyone else passed out in the luxurious seats around them. The private jet was one of the many things Ian and Devon had splurged on upon starting Trident Security. It sure as hell beat flying in the cargo transport planes that Jake and the other retired SEALs on board had spent countless hours in traveling around the world from one tour or mission to another.

"The head."

Jake closed his eyes again as Nick quietly made his way toward the back of the aircraft. This was the first time both teams had flown for a mission at the same time. While there were enough seats for everyone, the cabin was a little cramped with all those bodies. Ian, Devon, Brody, and Kip "Skipper" Morrison had spent the first few hours contacting operatives who could help and gathering intel. The rest had double-checked their gear, stowed the weapons in the jet's hidden compartments, and done everything else they could to prepare for the rescue. And, yes, it was still classified as a rescue operation and not a recovery one.

Thanks to a Christmas present Ian had given his mother years ago, they'd been able to zero in on where the two women had been taken to. The watch had a tracking device in it, not that Marie was aware of it. She probably would've thought her son was being paranoid and not worn the thing while traveling to some of the poorest areas around the globe to help children in need. Chuck had known, of course, and had also been gifted a similar watch. Even though the man always accompanied his wife abroad, he wasn't oblivious to the fact that due to his wealth, either one of them could become a target for ransom. He'd been at the helm of his real estate conglomerate for over thirty years, but over the past few years, he'd come to rely on his staff and executive board more and more. He didn't want to be one of those people who continually chased the almighty dollar without taking time to enjoy the fruits of his labor. He could fully retire tomorrow and still never have to worry about finances for the rest of his life. Hell, his grandchildren wouldn't have to worry about them for the rest of their lives, either.

Not long after takeoff, Brody had gotten on the phone with Jones in Scotland. He'd needed the other geek to hack into a satellite for him in case he lost track of the signal during their flight. They now had it pointed at the location where Marie Sawyer and, hopefully, the other woman were being held. The topographical images showed they were in a gated residential compound with a large house and several smaller buildings. Cook and Jones were in their respective war-rooms on either side of the pond, currently gathering all the intel they could about who owned the place. When the Steel team landed, they'd start reconnaissance and maintain a covert perimeter. Ian didn't want them going in without the Alpha and Omega teams unless it was absolutely necessary. While they all trusted Mic's operatives, it was best to have all available boots on the ground to make sure they rescued the women unharmed. Chuck and the people at the clinic still hadn't received a ransom demand, which wouldn't have been a surprise given the area and that Marie was an American physician. They had no idea why the two were taken and by whom, and there were too many variables to rush in without intel. Hopefully, by the time the TS jet landed, they would learn a lot more than they already knew.

About fifteen minutes passed before Jake realized Nick hadn't returned from the bathroom. Getting to his feet, he stretched and glanced toward the back of the cabin, catching just a glimpse of his husband standing off to the side in the small galley. Striding down the aisle, Jake passed the curtain that would afford them a little privacy and pulled it across the entryway. Nick leaned against a counter, staring down at his iPad. Jake put his back to a cabinet across from him—there were mere inches separating them. "What're you doing, babe?"

He tilted the screen so Jake could see it too. "Flipping through our wedding photos. Mom looked so—" He gulped. "So happy in every single one. It just hit me how much I've taken her for granted all these years. I thought she'd always be there for us, you know? To see Little Bit born, to see him or her and JD grow up... to see us have a kid someday."

Jake's eyebrows shot up. That last part had been

said in barely a whisper, choked with emotion. Taking the iPad from Nick, he set it on the counter behind him before closing the distance between them. Cupping Nick's jaw, Jake leaned down and kissed him. Neither of them had shaved since yesterday morning, so their whiskers rasped together sensuously. Not wanting to start something they couldn't finish and knowing he had to respond to Nick's last statement, Jake pulled back a little and stared down at his husband.

"She'll be there, Nick, for all those things. We'll get her back. She's not leaving us yet." He paused. "How long have you been thinking about having kids?"

Staring at Jake's chest, Nick shrugged. "A while now, I guess. You never brought the subject up, so I was sort of waiting for the right time. I mean, it's a huge step, one I never thought I'd take, but with JD and Mara around all the time and Angie about to give birth, I don't know… it's been on my mind a lot lately.

Jake smiled. "Yeah, well, you're not the only one. I didn't bring it up because I didn't have a good role model for a father—I'm not sure I'd be a good one. The thought of raising a kid kind of scares me a little."

That was an understatement. Throughout most of his childhood, Jake hadn't realized what an ass his father had been to him and his older brother, Mike.

The man had erected a wall between the two boys by favoring his younger son, who'd been a standout in many sports but none more than football, which had earned him a full ride to Rutgers University. But that all changed when the bigoted Sean Donovan found out Jake was homosexual during his senior year in high school. After trying to "beat the gay" out of his son to the point he needed two weeks to recover, the older man had lost him.

Hours after graduating, Jake enlisted in the Navy, throwing away his scholarship and any love or respect he'd ever had for his father. The two had barely said more than a dozen words to each other before Sean passed away years later. The only reason Jake had seen the man during that time was because of his mother and brother. It wasn't until recently that Jake and Mike buried the hatchet and were able to repair the damage their father had done to their relationship. Since joining SEAL Team Four and becoming close friends with Devon, Ian, and the rest of the Alpha team members, Jake felt Chuck Sawyer was more of a dad to him than his own father had ever been. Jake would lay down his life for his in-laws... and their sons.

Lifting his chin, Nick peered up at him. "Are you kidding? You'd make a great father, Jake. Besides JD and Mara, I've seen how you've taken care of Jenn and Alyssa. You're good with kids, no matter their age, whether you realize it or not."

Having been one of her many non-biological uncles from the teams, Jake had watched Jenn grow from a toddler to the beautiful young woman she'd become. Meanwhile, Alyssa was a teenager he'd rescued twice from an abusive father. Now that both her parents were dead, she was living with Boomer's parents, who'd become her legal guardians. Alyssa and Jake spoke over the phone or through texts several times a week. She was a good kid, and Jake was proud of how she was overcoming the horrors of being repeatedly raped by her father at a young age and having her mother killed by men who worked for the bastard. Thanks to Rick and Eileen Michaelson, though, she now had her GED and was enrolled in the nursing program at their community college.

"I don't know about that, but thanks to you, I'm willing to give it a go."

Nick's eyes widened. "Seriously? You're not just saying that to take my mind off Mom, are you?"

A playful frown appeared on his face as he squeezed Nick's shoulders. "What's our number one rule, subbie?"

In an instant, Nick willingly and naturally fell into the submissive role in their relationship. The younger man had never known he was a sub until the alpha in Jake had topped him. "Honesty, Sir."

"Exactly. So, I meant what I said. After we get your mom back to the States and all this chaos is over, we'll sit down and talk about our options. There's some stuff we'll have to change, though. We won't be able to go on the same assignments anymore, among other things."

It was weird. Now that the subject of having children had been brought up between them, Jake found he liked the idea a lot more than he had in the past. Maybe it was time to move on to the next chapter in their lives—the one where their family grew a little more.

CHAPTER SIX

Jenn hurried into the studio, shutting the door behind her. "Any news?"

Angie and Kristen had convinced her to go to work at her internship in the Tampa Social Services department for a few hours since there was nothing any of them could do but wait and worry. The heads of the Sawyer family weren't her biological grandparents, but she'd been calling them Grandpa and Grandma since she'd been a little girl. Her mother's and father's parents had all died before Jenn had reached the age of three, so Chuck and Marie had happily filled that void in her life for all these years.

"Not yet, sweetie," Fancy answered from her perch on the couch. "Grab a drink and a plate from the kitchen, and come have some pizza." She gestured to two opened boxes sitting on the coffee table between the group of women. From the looks of things, though, nobody had been really hungry, except maybe Mara, who was stuffing plain rotini pasta into her mouth, and JD, who had his fist in his mouth.

After a pit stop in the kitchen, Jenn joined everyone gathered in the sitting area, taking a seat next to Harper and sliding a cheese slice onto her plate. "What time are they supposed to land?"

"Not until around seven-thirty tonight, our time, which is seven-thirty in the morning there. Figuring that out is the easy part—just don't ask me what day it is over there—that always gets me all confused. Plus a day? Minus a day? Unless I'm making reservations somewhere, it doesn't make a bit of difference to me."

Jenn picked at her piece of pizza and glanced across the room to Kristen, who was talking on the phone. She didn't look happy. Her aunt slammed down the cordless receiver and strode toward them. Jenn's eyes widened. "What's wrong? What did I miss?"

Flopping into one of the recliners, Kristen grabbed her laptop from a side table. "Someone plagiarized *Hearts Ablaze*! I have to send proof that I hold the sole copyright to the book and other stuff. I don't know why they can't just look and see that I've had it published for years before this…" She furtively glanced at Mara. "… B-I-T-C-H came along. Shelby, can you use my desktop computer to take screenshots of both my book and the stolen version? I have to send them too—just the first few pages. I have to go through my files for the copyright and then write a Cease & Desist letter. Once I send them everything, and they see I'm telling the truth, they'll remove the other listing."

Jenn was appalled anyone would steal someone else's hard work and pass it off as their own, but it wasn't the first time she'd heard of it happening. She just felt bad that this time it'd been done to someone she loved—and at the worst possible time. With Marie missing, Kristen didn't need this right now. "Can I do anything to help?"

Kristen sighed, and her shoulders sagged. "After you eat, would you mind trying to get JD down for a nap?"

"Of course!" She loved the little boy she considered her nephew. His smile and dimples were the highlight of her day, every day.

"Thanks, I really appreciate it."

Twenty minutes later, Jenn had finished her lunch and JD was in a fresh diaper. Since he was a little fussy, Jenn put him in his stroller and took him for a walk around the compound, hoping the motion would lull him to sleep. Beau, of course, joined them. Ian's dog took his protective watch seriously. If JD was out and about, so was Beau, watching his six, as Jenn's uncles would say.

As she rounded the corner of the apartment building to stroll through Ian's Oasis, the beautiful yard Angie had created for him, Jenn groaned and wished she could turn around, but it was too late. Doug Henderson was headed her way and had already spotted her. It would make her look like the immature woman he thought she was if she turned around and pretended she hadn't seen him. That was the last thing she wanted. Ever since the one and only kiss she'd shared with the man, who was over seven years her senior, she wanted him more than ever. Unfortunately, he didn't feel the same way, and she'd embarrassed herself in front of him. Just the thought of how he'd turned her down after that amazing kiss made her blush. It was hot enough, though, so she could blame it on the sun.

Pasting on an expression of indifference, she tried to act like the sight of him wasn't breaking her heart. "Something wrong, Doug?"

He stopped in front of the stroller and gave the baby a quick smile. "Hey, kiddo." His gaze then flittered to Jenn. "No, nothing's wrong, at least not here. I'm heading over to the studio to check in with Kristen and Angie. The Steel Corps team landed in the Philippines and met up with Carter and Jordyn."

T. Carter and his girlfriend, Jordyn Alvarez, were good friends of Jenn's uncles. While they were introduced to most people as the executives of an import/export company, Jenn knew that wasn't true. She didn't know the extent of who they really were, but they were operatives for one of the US agencies.

She suspected the CIA or NSA but wasn't certain. All she *did* know was that if anyone at Trident needed them, the couple would be there in a heartbeat and vice versa. Carter had even helped rescue Jenn and Angie when they'd been taken hostage a few years ago.

"Do they know where Grandma Marie is yet?"

Doug hesitated, which made her stomach drop. But then he said, "I don't have all the details, but they've been able to track the signal from her watch to a residential area. We think she and the nurse are okay for now. I wish I could tell you more, but…"

"That's okay. I'm used to it." Her father had been on the same SEAL team as Ian, Devon, Brody, Jake, Marco, and Boomer. Between the seven of them, they had a lot of secrets about their classified missions that they couldn't tell anyone who didn't "need to know." She'd learned a long time ago she wouldn't get the details of any of their tours or assignments. Her parents had been killed because of one of those secrets during Jenn's senior year in high school. Since then, she'd been trying to deal with that fact as best she could.

"Well, at least I can give Kristen some good news." He held up a piece of paper. "With a little help from Nathan, I was able to figure out who her plagiarist is."

Jenn's eyes went wide. "Who?"

"Some twenty-three-year-old guy in Canada

pretending to be a woman. He's in a lot of author and reader groups on Facebook under his real name and has an author page under the fake one."

"Seriously? How'd you find that out?"

He shrugged and gave her a sheepish smile. "It was more Nathan's doing than mine. I just did what he told me to do and searched what he said to search. How he can work on more than one problem at a time is beyond me. The kid's a genius and deserves every penny the bosses pay him."

Jenn had no idea how much her uncles were paying Nathan, but it had obviously been enough to lure him into the private sector. He was also a really nice guy, just a couple of years older than her. When her e-reader had been giving her trouble recently, and Brody hadn't been around, Nathan had quickly fixed it for her.

"Will Kristen be able to sue him for any money he's gotten from the stolen book?"

"Yeah, but I'm not too sure it would be worth her time. Nathan had me use this tool that showed the rankings for the book since it was published, and at most, he only made about a hundred bucks or so. If he had a larger following, it might have been a different story."

JD started to fuss, so Jenn pushed the stroller back and forth. "So, he gets away with it?"

"That's up to her. I just checked, and all three of the guy's books are down. From what Kristen told me earlier, he'll probably get his entire account shut down too. My guess is he saw some scam post or something about how to publish books without writing them and make a lot of money doing it. I found a bunch of them while I was researching the guy. There's a scam for everything nowadays."

"Seems to be." Jenn scrambled to think of something else to say. Something that would keep Doug there, talking to her. This was the first real conversation they'd had since the kiss they'd shared, and she didn't want it to end. God, she was a hopeless romantic whose object of her affection wanted to be nothing more than friends, at the very most, and acquaintances who barely said hello to each other, at the very least.

In the uncomfortable silence that ensued, Doug glanced down at the stroller, then lowered his voice. "He's asleep."

Leaning forward, Jenn peered under the shade canopy. Sure enough, JD was out like a light, and that gave her an idea. "Great. I'll walk back to the studio with you. It's cooler in there for him." Anything to spend a few more minutes with the man who owned her heart—too bad he didn't want it.

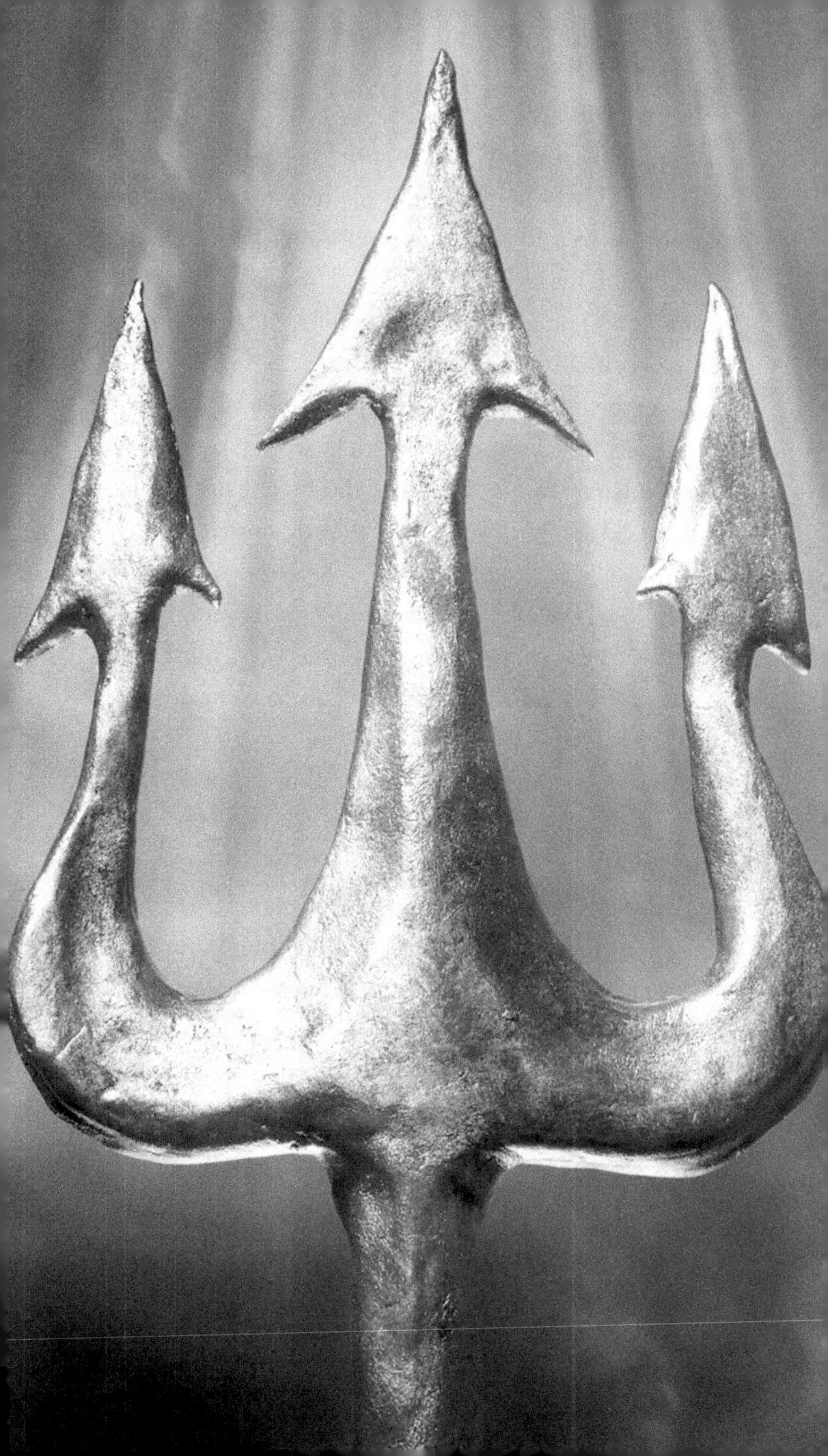

CHAPTER SEVEN

Thanks to T. Carter and his black-ops connections, the Trident Security teams landed at a covert US-Philippines allied military training base where they wouldn't have to deal with customs. They also wouldn't have to answer any questions about why they were there.

The jet taxied into a private hangar, where everyone began to disembark. Waiting for them were four nondescript vans, Chuck Sawyer, Pierce, Red, Carter, and Jordyn. The latter two were operatives of a clandestine US government agency, Deimos, and good friends of the original TS Alpha team. They were also a couple and had been the first two calls Ian had made after contacting his brothers, their team-mates, and the pilots. As per Carter's and Jordyn's system, he'd left voicemail messages for each, not knowing if they were together or not. Thankfully, they'd gotten back to him right away and had been somewhere close enough to get there before everyone else. There were very few people Ian trusted to keep his family safe, and most of them were now present.

Pierce and Red headed for the jet, pausing to shake hands with Ian, Devon, Nick, and Jake along the way, and joined the rest of the operatives unloading the go-bags, equipment, and weapons. Reaching the others, Ian approached his father first and pulled him into a hug. "We'll get her back, Dad."

"I know you will, son."

Devon embraced the Sawyer patriarch next. "Hey, Dad. How're you holding up?"

"A lot better now that you're all here." He glanced sheepishly at the couple standing nearby. "No offense to Carter, Jordyn, and the other team you sent, of course."

He squeezed his father's shoulder. "I'm sure there's none taken."

While Nick and Jake greeted Chuck, Ian turned his attention to the two Deimos spies. "Thanks for coming. Hope we didn't interrupt anything important."

Jordyn smiled and gave him a kiss on the cheek. "Nothing that can't wait, so no worries. I'm glad we could help—Marie means a lot to us."

That was their mom—she meant a lot to many people. Ian didn't think she'd ever met someone she didn't win over almost immediately. No matter how busy she was, she always gave everyone her utmost attention, making them feel they were the center of her world at that very moment. She was a great listener, and if anyone was special to her husband or her sons, they were special to her too, even if she'd just met them. This was not just an assignment to anyone there—it was to rescue a woman they all loved and respected.

Ian shook hands with Carter. "Got an updated sit-rep for us?"

"Yup, and you're not gonna like it. But let's get out of here first. We've got a few rooms at a hotel near the target site. Hopefully, we won't need them for long."

Giving Carter a curt nod, Ian fought the urge to tell him to spit out the intel. But the spy was right—this wasn't the place for it. They weren't on their home turf. The hotel would be more private—and they'd brought signal jammers with them to block any bugs or long-range listening devices. Being paranoid in their business was a good thing.

"Let's finish loading up and get going." He'd call Angie on the way to the hotel and let her know they'd arrived safely. He also wanted to make sure she hadn't gone into labor and not contacted him on the jet's phone for fear she'd worry him. If she was in labor, there wasn't a damn thing he could do about it from there. One of the hardest things he ever had to do was push his wife and unborn child to the back of his mind. Right then, though, he had to focus on rescuing his mother, the only other woman who could bring him to his knees.

A half hour later, they were gathered in one of the penthouse suites of the hotel. The décor was a little over the top, but it didn't matter. What *did* matter was there was plenty of room for them to prepare to go to war. And it was definitely a war they were heading into—those bastards had his mother, and hell was about to rain down on them.

Gathered in a combined dining/living area, they listened as Carter filled them in on his last conversation with Jones. He pointed to the image on the iPad Jordyn was holding up. "Crisanto de la Vega—runs the Davao del Norte division of the Barrera cartel."

There were a few muttered curses around the room. The Barrera cartel was to the Philippines what the Diaz cartel had been to South America. The head of that snake, Emmanuel Diaz, had been killed by his second-in-command, Felix Secada, before he, in turn, had been killed by Darius during an undercover op that had gone FUBAR. Darius had shoved Secada's nose into his brain while rescuing Princess Tahira who was now his new bride.

Ian was getting really sick of dealing with drug cartels. "What's that got to do with our mom?"

Swiping the screen, Jordyn brought up another image—this one was of an Asian man. "Xiao Zhihao —one of the Barrera's hitmen. MSS just bumped him up into their Top Ten Most Wanted." The Ministry of State Security was China's CIA counterpart.

Can this shit get any worse?

"Who do they suspect he killed?" Nick asked.

Standing with his arms crossed over his chest, Ian responded before anyone else could, "Kang Zhi, Chinese ambassador to Bahrain and reputed presidential candidate for the next election." It was a wild guess but an educated one. "Kang was shot and killed, along with one of his bodyguards, three nights ago. MSS has been holding back a lot of the intel from the press, and they've been trying to pass it off as a home invasion gone wrong."

Carter nodded. "You watch way too much CNN and BBC, dude, but you're right, as usual. During our recon of the compound earlier, Jordy got a glimpse of Xiao when he arrived at the compound late last night and recognized him."

"We've crossed paths before," the female spy added. Considering some of her assignments involved assassinations of foreign threats to the United States, it made sense she would recognize a peer, even if the man didn't have a conscience like she had. "I called a contact at MSS, and they confirmed, unofficially, of course, that a surveillance camera caught just enough of the assassin's face to verify it was Xiao."

"Okay, again, what does this have to do with our mom?" Nick interjected.

"Word is," Carter explained, "de la Vega has a state-of-the-art surgical suite at the compound."

Almost everyone in the room made the connection right away after hearing that, but it was Ian who spoke. "They needed a plastic surgeon to reconstruct Xiao's face so he's no longer recognizable."

"Yup. Apparently, the doc who'd done the last few surgeries for de la Vega, in exchange for canceling some of his gambling debts, got a little too greedy and tried to blackmail him and whomever he'd operated on. The doc's body was found not too long ago, missing both its hands and head." That wasn't an uncommon form of revenge in this region. "From the activity we observed at the compound, my guess is Marie will be doing the surgery sometime this morning." He slid a piece of paper into the middle of the table. "Here's the layout of the compound. We think this building here is where the surgical suite is located. Marie and the nurse, Jocelyn, are probably being held in the main house and treated well, although they most likely threatened Jocelyn to ensure Marie would do the procedure."

Studying the crudely sketched map, Ian pushed aside all thoughts of what his mother had to be going through and began doing one of the things he did best—formulating a plan of attack with a take-no-prisoners strategy. The clock was ticking.

CHAPTER EIGHT

Chuck sat on one of the living room chairs, then popped right back up again. He was slowly going crazy. His sons and their friends and teammates had left an hour ago in broad daylight, although they would've preferred it had been under the cloak of darkness. Their plan was to infiltrate the compound where Marie and Jocelyn were being held any minute now. Devon had explained to him that the best time to attack the enemy was in the wee hours of the morning. If they weren't already asleep, their guards would be down—boredom and exhaustion made a person's reaction time much slower. Unfortunately, they didn't think Marie and Jocelyn had until the morning to be rescued. There was a strong possibility the two women would be killed after the surgery since they could identify both Xiao and de la Vega.

"The waiting is almost as bad as the worry, isn't

it?" CC Chapman asked as he exited one of the pent-house's bedrooms and stretched. The aviator had taken the opportunity to take a shower after spending over eighteen hours in the jet's cockpit. His co-pilot had stayed with the aircraft in the private hangar to make certain it was properly refueled and nobody messed with it.

"Pretty much. I just made a new pot of coffee—help yourself."

"Thanks."

As the retired Air Force pilot shuffled into the kitchen, Chuck sat down again and turned on the volume of the muted television. He had no idea what the CNN newscaster was reporting, nor did he care—it just gave the room some white noise to distract him from his worst thoughts.

Even without their specialized training, Chuck knew his sons would do everything possible to rescue their mother. While he'd wanted to be there when Marie was brought safely from the compound, he understood he would've just been in the way. To kill some time, he'd called the main offices of Operation Smile and given them an update. When he'd spoken to them yesterday, after talking to Ian, he'd asked directors to keep the news of the missing women quiet for now. At first, they'd objected, but once he'd explained who his sons were and what they were going to do, they'd relented and agreed it was in the women's best interest for the rescue to be done under the radar.

Chuck couldn't imagine life without his beloved wife. They'd seemed like a mismatched couple when they'd first met. With only an associate degree in business administration, Chuck had followed his mother's footsteps into real estate. When he'd been younger, and money had been tight at times, she'd taken him on many of her appointments, showing prospective buyers the local listings. Somewhere along the line, Chuck had become a bit of a salesman in his own right during those times. He'd tell young parents or newlyweds about how the backyard of a certain house was a great place for kids or other things like that.

The night he'd met the woman who would become his wife, Marie O'Toole had been out with friends, enjoying a brief period of downtime in between her four years of medical school and starting her residency. He'd been out celebrating closing on the most recent property he'd sold as a real estate agent—it'd been his first seven-figure sale, which had netted him a hefty commission. Chuck had seen the lovely doctor across the bar room and had fallen in love. By the end of the night, he'd convinced her to have coffee with him the next day. That'd been the start of their budding romance, which was still going strong to this very day.

While they'd had their ups and downs, as every couple did, their marriage had thrived as she'd become one of the top plastic surgeons in North Carolina, and he'd invested well in real estate and had created a billion-dollar empire. It had all started with a foreclosed apartment building he'd bought two years before their first son had been born. Sawyer-O'Toole was now one of the biggest corporate, commercial, and residential real estate firms on the East Coast. But Chuck and Marie had never taken their wealth for granted and refused to let their sons do that either.

After welcoming Ian, their firstborn, into the family, Devon and then John followed. Nick, the youngest, had been a pleasant surprise for the couple, after several years of thinking they wouldn't have any more children. Nick was six years old when Ian left to join the Navy after his high school graduation. Despite having trust funds set up for his boys, Chuck had insisted each one get either a four-year college degree or spend that time in a branch of the military. While they'd gotten a small stipend from their trusts, between their teens and twenties, they didn't get to manage their own accounts until they'd reached thirty. Well, that had been true for Ian and Devon. When twenty-seven-year-old Nick had gotten married to Jake a few months ago, Chuck had gifted his youngest son full control of his trust.

As for John, Chuck's heart still squeezed when he thought of his third oldest son. Somehow, as close as their family had been and still were, they'd all missed the signs that the senior in high school had developed a severe drinking problem. Others might ask, "How could you not know what was going on under your own roof?" But, like most alcoholics, John had become adept at hiding his addiction. By the time his parents had found out about it, it'd been too late.

Chuck would never forget that fateful day. Marie had been at her private practice; Ian had been on the other side of the world; Devon had been away at college; and little Nick had been in elementary school. It'd happened only a few days after the Christmas/New Year's break. John was supposed to have been in class, too, but for whatever reason, he'd returned home after everyone else had left for the day. He'd gotten drunk, vomited, and then aspirated, dying two full hours before Chuck had swung by the house to get some papers he'd forgotten. He'd found his son unresponsive on the kitchen floor, and despite his efforts to revive him, when the paramedics responded, they'd gently told a devastated Chuck there wasn't anything they could do to save his boy. Rigor mortis had already begun to set in. One and a half empty bottles of vodka had been found, and when the coroner's report came back, it'd stated John's alcohol level had been four times the legal limit. Over the next few days, while waiting for Ian to fly back to the States for the funeral, Dev had learned from John's friends the extent of his alcoholism.

Out of the three grieving brothers, Devon had taken it the hardest. With his parents' blessing, he'd dropped out of college and enlisted. John had talked about following Ian into the Navy, and Dev had decided to do it since his brother was no longer able to. Whether he'd joined the Navy for the right reasons or not was no longer a question in anyone's mind. A few years after enlisting, Dev had achieved his ultimate goal, surviving the BUD/s training and securing a spot on SEAL Team Four with his brother and the men who were now still fighting by his side.

Chuck glanced at his watch. Wow, a full two minutes had passed. The wait was going to drive him mad. Feeling helpless, he wished there was something he could do. Earlier, he'd gone with Devon and Marco to retrieve his and Marie's bags and things from the little hostel they'd been staying in for the past few weeks. As soon as the teams got the two women out of there, they'd take Jocelyn wherever she wanted to go, then head to the airport. If things went to shit, Ian wanted everyone in the air before the authorities found out. Knowing how the teams worked, Chuck was certain they'd leave no evidence of their identities behind. If God forbid, the authorities found out who'd been involved, well, let's just say it was a good thing Ian had the assistant director of the FBI on speed dial, among other people with high government clearances. While the Government of the Philippines would probably be thrilled if one of their notorious drug lords ended up dead, Chuck wasn't too sure how they'd feel about a rogue team dispensing justice.

Standing, he strode toward the doors leading to a balcony and then stepped out into the heat. High above, the sun beat down as it peaked for the day. With a sigh, he counted the seconds until he'd see the woman he treasured more than anything else in the world again—his beautiful Marie.

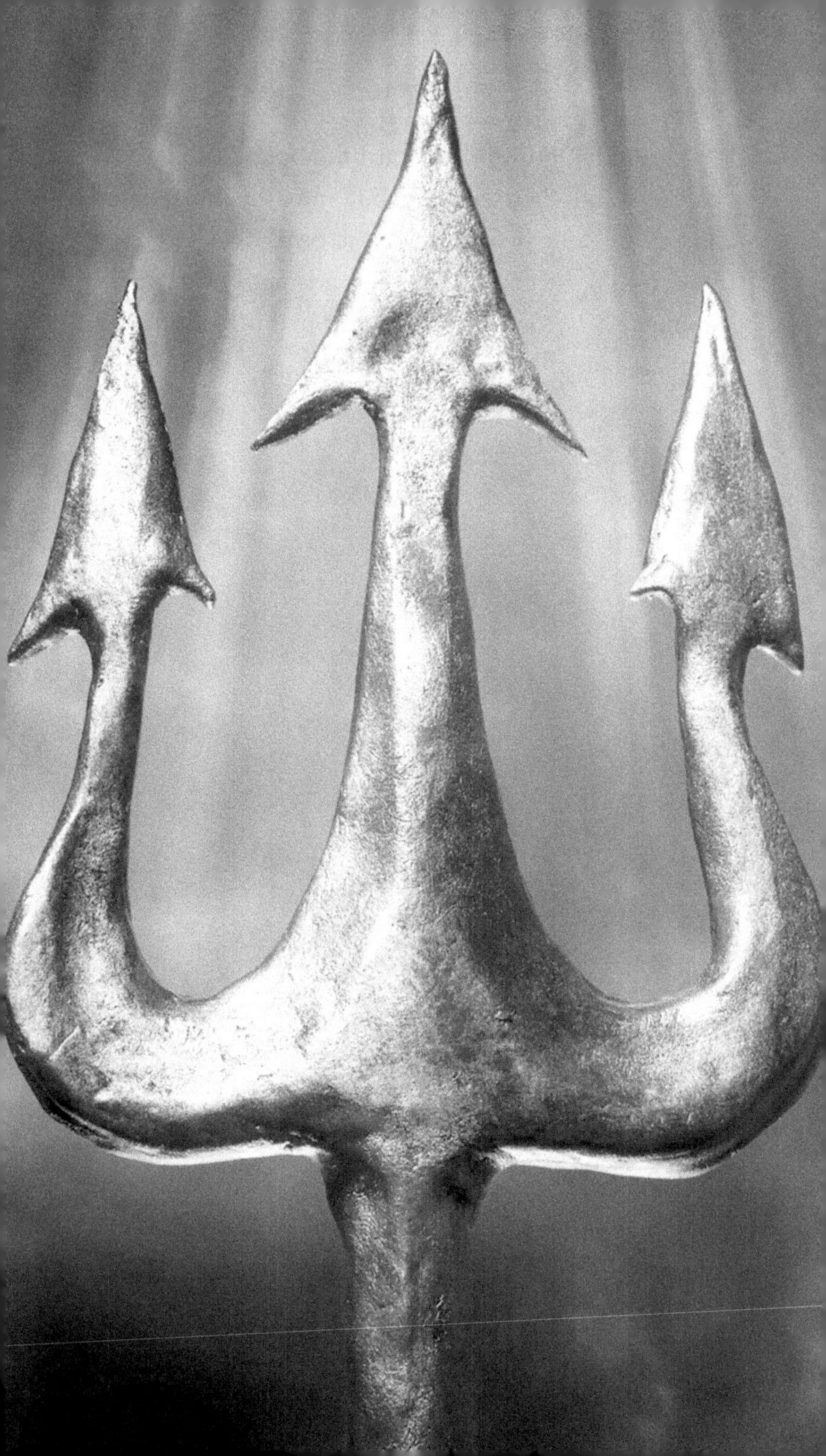

CHAPTER NINE

Marie glanced around the guarded, walled-in compound as she and Jocelyn followed Albano from the main house across a well-maintained lawn with beautiful landscaping—another sign of his wealth. They approached a small building that appeared to have been made with thick concrete blocks and had no windows she could see. Bringing up the rear were Antonio and another goon, as Ian would probably call him—either that or one of his favorite "twat" words. She couldn't wait until his child was old enough to start repeating everything he said —Marie was going to just sit back and laugh. Although she usually rebuked her sons whenever they cursed in her presence, she knew it came with the territory of being a Navy SEAL and private security operative. Once you're exposed to something, over time, it tends to become a habit. And, sometimes, a situation just called for a swear word or two.

Everyone at Trident was trying to curb their foul language by having a "curse jar" on Colleen's desk, but whenever Marie had been visiting and seen it, the darn thing was always full of $10 bills. She'd bet anything most of it had come from Ian. At least the money was going to a good cause, helping veterans with PTSD get support dogs.

One of Marie's other acts of charity, which her sons didn't know about, although Chuck did, was performing facial reconstructive surgery on veterans who'd served in Iraq and Afghanistan and been disfigured from shrapnel or bullets. Many of them couldn't afford it, and military benefits only went so far, so she donated her time and expertise through a non-profit organization one of her medical school friends had founded a few years ago after her own daughter had been injured in combat. It was Marie's way of paying it forward since Ian, Devon, Nick, and their teams had survived their tours relatively intact—aside from Ian taking a bullet to the chest during an ambush while still in the Navy. Marie did the surgeries in honor of God or the powers that be who hadn't taken another one of her children. Losing John had devastated her family, and Marie never wanted another one of her sons to die before her. No parent should have to go through that, but, unfortunately, it'd happened, and despite her grief, she'd remained strong for her husband and surviving sons—especially Nick, who'd still been in elementary school at the time. And, now, she would stay strong until her "boys" came to her rescue—that included all the Trident operators, counting Lindsey, who she doubted would take offense at the informal male moniker. Marie would do what she had to in order for her and Jocelyn to remain alive. If that meant performing surgery under duress, so be it.

The thought of doing a lousy job on whoever was going under the knife had crossed her mind a few times since last night, but her personal and professional codes of ethics wouldn't let her. That didn't mean she wouldn't take her time and be very meticulous about the reconstruction, giving Ian and Devon's teams a chance to find her and Jocelyn. Marie wasn't as naive as her eldest son thought she was—she knew there was a tracking device inside the watch he'd given her many Christmases ago. She didn't doubt for a second Brody had a satellite pinpointing her location right now. Thank God for technology!

Stopping in front of a door, Albano punched a few numbers on a keypad beside it until there was a click. Pulling the door open, he led them inside. The sterility of the sparse building surprised her. Albano paused and gestured down a hallway that seemed to run the length of the building. "Aside from the operating room, there's a pre- and post-op room, a scrub room, and a radiology room. My staff has already obtained the X-rays you'll need. If you follow me, I'll introduce you to your patient. You'll have silicone implants and all the necessary tools to alter his face at your disposal."

As Jocelyn walked next to her, Marie was glad to see the woman had regained her composure and emotional strength. They'd sat in the bedroom for several hours yesterday, watching TV, eating the meals they'd been served, and talking. The longer they'd chatted about everything under the sun and watched a few old movies, the calmer Jocelyn had become. Whispering under the raised volume of the television, in case the room was bugged, Marie had explained who her sons were and that they'd be coming to the rescue. All she and Jocelyn had to do was get through the surgery and act normal—whatever normal was under the circumstances.

Albano had wanted Jocelyn to wait in the main house while Marie performed the surgery, but she'd insisted her nurse assist her, explaining they'd done many procedures and worked well together. The physician had been shocked when their unwanted host had relented, however, he'd required his two nurses observe the surgery to make certain the doctor was doing her job properly. A nurse anesthetist would also be present. Marie would've preferred an anesthe-siologist, but she'd deal with it.

When they entered what apparently was the pre- and post-op room, Marie caught the first sight of her patient and breathed a small sigh of relief she didn't recognize the Asian man. If she'd known who he was, that would probably have increased their odds of not getting out of this mess alive. He was sitting on a reclining chair next to a gurney, surrounded by the state-of-the-art equipment Albano had crowed about. The man was wearing dark gray dress pants, a white, button-down shirt with the sleeves rolled up to his elbows, and spit-shined, black leather oxfords. There was an air of importance combined with a sense of evil Marie felt emanating from him, and a shiver went down her spine.

Suck it up, Marie. You graduated at the top of your classes from high school all the way through medical school, you toughed it out when that pervy asshole, Dr. Branson, tried to make your life hell during your residency, you've given birth to four sons over nine pounds each, and you survived John's death—you're strong, and you can do this. Just give Ian, Devon, Nick, Jake, and everyone else time to come to the rescue. They'll be here soon. Just do what you must until then.

The internal pep talk helped, and the butterflies in her stomach calmed. Working under stressful conditions wasn't anything new to Marie, but this was the first time she was doing it while surrounded by men with guns.

Off to the left side of the unidentified man, two Filipino women stood silently, a prepped tray-table, with supplies to start an intravenous line, was between them. Both dressed in blue scrubs, these had to be the nurses, unless one was the anesthetist. To the right, another Asian man, this one tall, muscular, and wearing a suit, was standing sentry in the corner of the room, the big, black gun on his hip couldn't be missed—obviously a bodyguard. It made sense since the patient would be unconscious during the surgery.

"Dr. Sawyer, this is Mr. Wang," Albano said, indicating the seated man as if introducing them at a social gathering. He didn't bother introducing the two women or the man standing guard.

Marie fought the urge to roll her eyes—Wang was as common a surname in China as Smith or Albano were in the US and the Philippines, respectively. The man scrutinized her from head to toe, his glare hard and unemotional. After a few moments of silence, his gaze flitted to Albano, and he said something she didn't understand in Mandarin or Cantonese.

"Oh, I don't think you have anything to worry about, Mr. Wang," her captor replied in English with an amused lilt. "Dr. Sawyer is a well-respected surgeon in her country. She also knows if she makes even the slightest error during the procedure, she and her friend here will not survive the day."

What an idiot! Sure, make the doctor nervous going into surgery, you brilliant twat. Oh, God, Ian is rubbing off on me! Although that might not be a bad thing at the moment.

With her most professional facial expression and tone of voice, Marie took a step forward. "I assure you, Mr. Wang, even though I'm performing this surgery under duress, I will do my best. Blame it on my Hippocratic oath."

His response was an obnoxious *harrumph* before he spoke in his native language again. She looked to Albano to translate. He nodded at her. "You may proceed, Dr. Sawyer."

She surveyed the room. From an IV pole, hung a fresh bag of saline solution, ready to be hooked up to the patient after a line was started in his arm. An EKG monitor sat on a platform behind Wang with an attached blood pressure cuff. A folded, green hospital gown was draped over the back of the recliner. To Marie's right, on the wall, was an X-ray view box with three films tucked under the grip bar at the top. It looked like any other aseptic pre-op room she'd been in during her career, with a few obvious exceptions, such as there was only room for one patient.

And don't forget the guys with guns.

She pushed that unwanted last thought from her mind. "I hope you have scrubs for me and Jocelyn to change into—what we're wearing isn't exactly sterile."

"Of course, forgive me. You'll find them in the scrub room." Albano gestured toward a door to her left. Through its small window, she could see another door beyond it, which had to go into the operating room. "There's also a comfort room where you can change."

Marie almost thanked the man out of being polite, which was second nature to her, but she bit her tongue instead. She nodded to Jocelyn. "Let's go change, then I'll evaluate our patient." Before following her to the door, Marie turned to the other nurses. "Do you both speak English?"

"Yes," the shorter of the two replied. Unlike Marie and Jocelyn, neither appeared to be there against their will. If she had to guess, they were being paid very well for participating and maintaining their silence about what took place within their employer's compound. In this poor area of the world, money was scarce and could buy someone's cooperation in a heartbeat.

"Please get him changed into the gown, then take his vital signs and start the IV. I also want to speak to the anesthetist before he or she administers any drugs." The last thing she needed was a screw-up on that end.

"He's setting up in the OR."

Marie acknowledged the woman with a curt nod, then followed Jocelyn into the scrub room. Both had taken quick showers in their bathroom earlier but had needed to dress in the clothes they'd been wearing for the past twenty-five hours.

After opening a few cabinets, they found what they needed. Jocelyn used the half-bath first to change into a set of scrubs, and then Marie did the same. Folding her clothing, she left everything on top of Jocelyn's small pile on a stool but tucked her watch in the small back pocket of the scrub pants. Stepping back out of the windowless room, she joined Jocelyn at the basin sink. Using the provided foam antibacterial soap, they scrubbed their nail beds, hands, and arms. Marie would do it again right before starting the surgery, but it was a stall tactic no one should question. In her heart, she knew her boys were closing in on her location—she just had to hold it together until they got there.

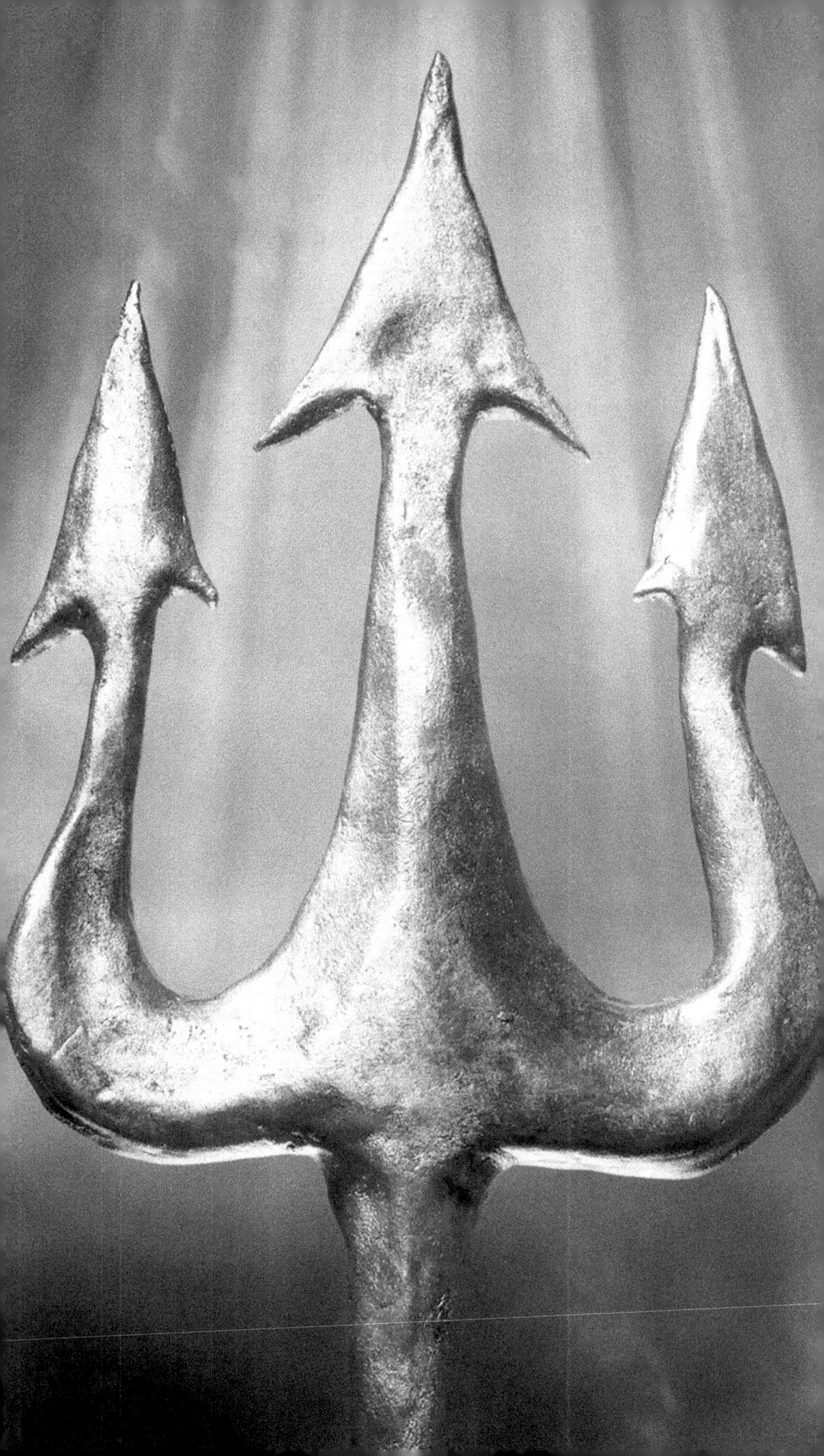

CHAPTER TEN

They had the compound partially surrounded, just waiting for the "go" signal, as the teams hid behind trees, shrubbery, rocks, and underbrush. Brody had hacked into the surveillance system and had most of the camera feeds now playing on loops, so the raiders wouldn't be spotted until it was too late. The main gate was guarded, and there were two men patrolling the grounds. The members of Steel had confirmed Marie and Jocelyn had been escorted, about an hour ago, to the building they suspected housed the surgical suite. There was no doubt in Devon's mind his mother would do everything in her power to stay alive until help arrived. He hoped she had faith in them finding her since, as far as he knew, she wasn't aware of the tracker in her watch.

Donning a disguise and using a fake ID, complete with a helicopter pilot's license in the same name, a burner credit card, and a large amount of cash, Marco had taken Red and Lindsey and rented a Bell B206 JetRanger. The female sharpshooter would cover their asses from above while Red flew the bird and Marco provided intel on the tangos' movements. The other available snipers, Jake, Carter, and Jordyn, were perched in trees, with the best views inside the compound, with their high-powered rifles.

When Ian gave the signal, Boomer and Pierce, Steel's EOD man, would set off explosives, which were attached to the walls on either side of the compound, blowing holes in the rock that others would use to enter. They both had a few frag grenades to further induce mayhem. Devon, Ian, Nick, and Brody were designated as Alpha Team, taking the east side, while Foster, Morrison, Reese, and Mancini, Omega Team, were on the west side. Meanwhile, two vans they'd rented, again with fake IDs, would storm the front gate, and the operatives inside, McCabe, Rook, Flynn, and Chris Jordon, would take down as many of the guards as they could while creating as much chaos for the enemy as they could. The goal was to be in and out in under eight minutes—anything longer than that, they'd have to deal with a local police response.

Unfortunately, they had to do this in broad daylight, so the more distractions they provided, the better chance they had of rescuing the principles without harm. They had no idea how long the doctor and nurse duo would remain alive after the completion of the surgery, which should last several hours. Devon hated thinking of his mother as an unnamed entity, but when a mission was personal, it had a higher chance of going FUBAR, and this one was fucked up enough already.

There was no way in hell Devon or his brothers were leaving this hellhole without their mother. She still had a lot of living to do, along with spoiling the crap out of her grandkids. Whenever she called to say hello, Devon would put the phone to his son's ear, and he was sure JD recognized his grandmother's voice because his face would light up, and he'd start cooing to her. Devon swore the next time they did that, he was going to use his Go-Pro to record it. When his mother did leave this Earth in another twenty or thirty years, if Devon's prayers that she lived a long time came true, he wanted lots of video and voice recordings of her so his and his brothers' future children, Little Bit, and JD had plenty to remember her by. But, damn it, today was not the day Marie Sawyer was going to meet her maker.

About an hour, give or take a few minutes, after he'd led the women into the surgical building, de la Vega had returned to the main house. So, unless there was a secret tunnel or someone had been in there longer than the Steel operatives had been keeping surveillance, there were only eight people in the smaller structure other than the two principals.

They'd seen two women and a man go inside, who they suspected were nurses or medical assistants, as well as Xiao, his bodyguard, and three of de la Vega's armed men. With any luck, the latter would come out to see what was going on when the pandemonium started and be taken down quickly. Xiao should be unconscious, leaving only his bodyguard and the surgical staff left to deal with.

"Bravo Team, you ready?" Ian asked over the comm system.

"Affirm," was Marco's reply.

"Omega Team?"

Foster's voice sounded in Devon's ear. "Ready."

"Echo One & Two?"

Boomer and then Pierce confirmed they were also primed and waiting.

"Charlie Team?"

"Ready," responded McCabe.

"Alpha Team is ready," Ian announced. "Everyone else, wait for the gate crashers. Charlie, on my mark—three… two… one… go!"

From a quarter of a mile up the road that the compound was on, the two white vans head toward their target like they were just out for a Sunday drive. A few moments passed before Devon could hear them approach and then accelerate. A split second before the first vehicle crashed into the wrought-iron gate, ripping it from its hinges and demolishing it, through their earpieces, they all heard, "Cowabunga!"

"Fucking Flynn," a few team members muttered as the explosives blew and all hell broke loose.

———

"How're his vitals?" Marie asked the Russian anesthetist as she prepared to make a small incision on the inside of Wang's right cheek. After changing into scrubs, she'd taken about twenty minutes to interview and examine her patient. Then, she'd scrutinized the x-rays, discussed the reconstruction options with him, and mapped out the changes she would make and where her incisions would be by using a surgical marker on his face. That had taken another forty minutes or so, and she was proud of herself for pretending this was any other day back at the hospital where she maintained her practicing privileges in Charlotte.

A few minutes into the physical exam, it'd become clear to her that, although he'd said he lacked formal medical training, Albano knew what he was talking about when it came to the procedures. To her surprise, he'd hung on her every word and had even made a few suggestions of his own. This wasn't the first reconstruction he'd been involved in. However, as they'd prepared to start the surgery, instead of staying and watching as she'd thought he would, he'd disappeared, leaving Antonio and Wang's bodyguard behind to make sure Marie didn't do anything stupid.

She'd been instructed to change the shape of Wang's jawline, cheeks, nose, chin, and forehead. The first three features required her to access the bones through incisions inside his mouth so she could shave and move the bones to alter their shape. The chin, forehead, and nostril area of the nose would get silicone injections. The final combination was not one she would choose for any of her patients for aesthetic reasons, but it wasn't her call. Even though she'd do her best, she honestly didn't care what the bastard looked like when it was all over.

While injecting silicone under the skin sounded simple enough to most people, it called for a physician who knew what they were doing to avoid disfigurement or nerve damage. Also, it was a slow process to ensure the skin looked smooth and natural after the post-operative swelling went down. With that and the contouring of the facial bones, they could be here for up to seven or eight hours. Since no one was insisting she hurry up, it was obvious they knew what she was doing was quite tedious. Again, that was something in her and Jocelyn's favor.

While Wang was asleep, he wasn't completely unconscious, which would've required him to be intubated. But that was impracticable since she needed access to the interior of his mouth for the jaw and cheeks. Instead, between the lidocaine injections she'd given him to numb his face and the sedation cocktail the anesthetist had administered, Wang was resting peacefully. While it might take a bit to rouse him without giving him another drug to counteract the first ones, he could still wake up on his own with enough non-pharmaceutical stimulation.

So far, Marie had completed working on her patient's nose, shaving down the slight bump in his cartilage and injecting a small amount of silicone to alter the shape of the nostrils just a bit. Although Jocelyn's hand shook at the start of the procedure, she'd quickly fallen into the familiar routine of assisting the surgeon. The other two nurses stood by and assisted efficiently enough when Marie asked them to. The unnamed bodyguard was also in the sterile surgical suite, wearing a mask and scrubs over his clothing, but he'd refused to cover up the holstered gun at his hip. Meanwhile Antonio had stayed in the pre-op room doing who knew what.

As she shifted to get the correct angle she needed, the floor shook under her feet, and Marie's hands froze. The tremor didn't last long, but it'd still been noticeable. And she wasn't the only one who'd felt it because everyone else was glancing around, wide-eyed. Since there were no windows anywhere in the building, they couldn't see outside, nor could they hear anything through the thick walls. The body-guard's eyes narrowed, and he stepped over to an intercom on the wall next to the door. Pushing a button, he asked, "What was that?"

Antonio's voice came through the small white box.

"Don't know. Probably a small earthquake. We get them all the time."

The bodyguard glared at Marie, evidently frowning despite his mask, then pushed the button again. "Confirm it."

A bored sigh preceded one word. "Fine."

The hair on the back of Marie's neck became energized, sending a shiver down her spine. That hadn't been any earthquake. She'd bet a million dollars that whatever had shaken the ground had been at the hands of Boomer, Trident's explosive ordinance disposal technician. Her boys were here, but she had to keep working like nothing was wrong until they got into the building and took out the bodyguard, who'd moved closer to Jocelyn, his weapon now in hand.

Taking a deep breath, Marie tilted her head from side to side, working out a few kinks that'd settled in her neck. Wang was still asleep, but every now and then, his hand with the inserted IV catheter would twitch, letting her know he wasn't completely under. Knowing she had to do something, otherwise the bodyguard would get suspicious—more than he already was—Marie made a small incision on the inside of Wang's cheek. If, in fact, she'd been wrong, and that *had* been a minor earthquake, she'd keep praying and waiting. Her boys would be here soon.

CHAPTER ELEVEN

Stacked, one behind the other, a short distance from the C4 Boomer had set against the wall, Ian, Devon, Nick, and then Brody waited as a huge hole was punched through the stone barrier. A second after the explosion, Ian led the charge, bursting through the smoke into the compound. On the other side of the massive backyard, Foster was doing the same with the Omega Team. At first, there were no tangos in sight, but Ian knew that wouldn't last for long. His legs quickly burned up the distance to the surgical building, keeping the sights of his AR-15 in line with where his gaze was directed.

From the front of the property, short bursts of gunfire resounded, but Ian trusted everyone on his teams were the ones who were still standing. Move-ment to his right had him swiveling in that direction, and he and Devon both fired their weapons after affirming the man with an assault rifle was a threat. The tango's body danced unnaturally with the impacts, and his finger squeezed the trigger of his gun, sending bullets flying harmlessly into the earth. Ian didn't pause, even for a split second, knowing the man wouldn't be getting back up.

By the time he got to the target building, three more tangos in the backyard were dead with their weapons beside them—all taken out by the snipers in the trees. Foster and the Omega Team lined up on one side of the only door while the Alpha Team fell to the other. Since the hinges were closer to Foster, and the door swung outward, that meant he would be opening it while Ian would be going in first. Devon would be right on his six. Mancini and Reese were facing the rest of the compound, covering everyone's asses. Those who were going into the building switched to the more accurate 9mm or 40 caliber pistols they were carrying. They needed the extra control in the close space to avoid shooting any innocent people.

Once everyone was ready, Nick took two steps out from the building and aimed his weapon so that if anyone was waiting for them on the other side of the door, he would have an immediate shot. Ian nodded to Foster, who reached for the handle, but the door flew open before he had a chance to grab it. An armed man stormed out, and a startled expression flashed on his face. Evidently, he hadn't expected to run into them. He had no time to raise the pistol in his hand as Nick fired one shot between his eyes, dropping him like a sack of sand.

Again, Ian knew they didn't have to worry about the dead man, so once Nick told him it was safe to enter, he stepped over the body without a second thought. The eight men quickly cleared the rooms as they made their way down the hall. When they got to the last closed door, Ian peeked through its small window, and he felt a measure of relief, as small as it was. His mother was in the middle of the surgery. Aside from the unconscious patient, there were three other women in the room and two men, one of whom appeared to be their main threat, given the fact he had a gun in his hand. When the guard's head turned toward the door, Ian ducked back out of sight. Using the hand signals they all knew, he passed on the intel to his teams and then assigned details.

Following the silent order, Foster and Mancini dropped down, low-crawled under the window, and popped up on the other side. Placing his hand on the door handle, Foster turned it ever so slightly, then nodded at Ian. Thank God it was unlocked.

Through their earpieces, they heard the snipers and other team members clearing the rest of the property. The thick concrete walls of the building muted the gunfire—at least in there. Outside was a different story. They had to hurry this up because the cops would be on their way soon.

Using three fingers, Ian counted down. When his hand became a fist, Foster pushed down on the handle and shoved the door open in a smooth movement. Before the guard could react, Ian put a bullet in his chest to the left of the sternum. Behind him, Devon fired a shot, and the other man dressed in scrubs hit the floor. He'd been at the head of the patient and tried to draw a gun from under a piece of equipment. Yeah, that didn't work out for him.

All four women had let out short screams. Wide-eyed, two of them raised their hands in the air and spoke in rapid Cebuano behind their surgical masks. While it wasn't one of the few languages Ian spoke, he knew enough to tell them not to move and keep their hands where he could see them. With his weapon pointed at both of them, Ian stepped to the side. "Egghead, search them."

Ian recognized his mother immediately, even behind the mask, scrubs, and cap, so the other woman who was practically clinging to her had to be the missing nurse, Jocelyn.

"Thank God you got here." Quickly regaining her composure, Marie dropped the instrument she'd been holding onto a surgical tray and then gestured to her patient. "I'm sure someone is looking for him."

She pushed a monitor out of the way and bent down to check the pulse of the man Devon had shot in the head. Seeing there was nothing she could do for him, she hurried over to the guard and did the same. But for him, she reached up and grabbed a pair of scissors off the tray and began cutting open his shirt. Foster watched her for a moment, then leaned toward Ian. "Is she seriously trying to save him?"

Ian sighed. "As serious as her Hippocratic oath."

After checking for a pulse and respiration and examining the man's bare chest and pupils, she pulled down her mask and announced, "He's dead."

"A bullet to the heart will do that, Ma. Now, if you're done trying to save the bastards who kidnapped you, can we get the hell out of here?"

"In a minute. Jocelyn, grab our clothes while I counteract the sedation on our patient and take out his IV." She searched another tray set up at the head of the gurney and selected two syringes. "Don't look at me like that, Nick. You did your job, now I'm doing mine. If you want to restrain him, might as well do it before he wakes up."

The youngest Sawyer shook his head, then glanced at Devon and Ian, neither of whom expected any less from their mother despite the fact she'd been abducted and forced to perform surgery on an assassin. As Dev simply pulled a zip-tie out of a pocket of his BDUs, Ian rolled his eyes and then activated the microphone attached to his earpiece. "Sit-rep."

Jake was in command outside. "All tangos down

for the count. Three female civilians secured. Clock's ticking."

"Copy that. Two female civilians in here too. Let them go." The grease paint the operatives had on their faces would protect their identities, although he expected the women would hightail it out of there and deny ever being present. "We'll be out of here in one. Jackass and Sweetheart, let your friends know you have a delivery for them."

Carter and Jordyn would make sure Xiao was turned over to the MSS for killing the Chinese ambassador. The female Deimos spy responded, "No problem, Boss-man."

On the gurney, the assassin was awake enough for them to drag his ass out of there without having to carry him, but he still didn't comprehend his predicament. Devon and Nick got him up and between the two of them.

Ian eyed his mother as she took her clothes from Jocelyn. "Let's get going. Dad's a mess waiting for you."

She chuckled. "Now you know where all of you get your calm demeanors from—me. Take me home, boys."

———

ANGIE BLINKED A FEW TIMES AS SHE BECAME FULLY awake. Her bedroom was dark, but enough moonlight peeked around the corners of the blinds for her to see. Glancing at the clock, she noted the time. 2:01 a.m. She'd only been asleep about three hours. While most of her girlfriends and family had gone home, Harper and Mara slept in her guest room. Meanwhile, Jenn had crashed upstairs in Kristen's apartment, even though hers was only a twenty-second walk to the other side of the building. Ian's goddaughter wanted to be close when the call came in about Marie.

The last thing they heard when Ian and Devon called to check in was that they knew where Marie was being held, and they would stage a daylight raid. Angie knew they preferred to do those at nighttime for the additional coverage and that their enemy would be slacking or asleep, so there had to be a valid reason for going in during the middle of the day. Whatever it was, she was sure it wasn't good. She still didn't know why Marie and her friend had been abducted in the first place, other than it wasn't for ransom, and that, of course, sent her mind in a tail-spin, wondering what the reason was.

Pressure was building on her bladder, so she squirmed toward the edge of the bed. Usually, Ian was there to help her up—he was such a light sleeper, and she woke him all the time despite her attempts not to. His sleep had been as disrupted as hers during the last few weeks.

Once her legs were hanging over the side, she slowly rolled up into a sitting position and felt a sharp pain in her lower abdomen. She'd been having them off and on again since shortly after Ian had left, and Kristen and their shared obstetrician had assured her they were nothing to worry about. Braxton Hicks contractions were irregular and far less intense than true contractions—Kristen had spoken from experience. She and Devon had run to the hospital twice before JD had been born, only to get sent home. Angie's poor brother-in-law had been more stressed out over that than his wife had been. Ian swore he wasn't going to act like a lunatic when Angie finally went into labor, but right then, she wished he would—it would mean he was here with her, running around like a chicken without its head.

Waddling to the bathroom, she emptied her bladder, then flushed and washed her hands. As she turned toward the doorway, a piercing pain struck her lower back and then radiated to the front as the contraction started.

She grasped the door jamb and bent over as much as possible, which wasn't a lot. "Holy shit!"

It was much harder than any of the other contractions she'd had. She moaned until the pain began to recede again. It hadn't been as strong or as long as she'd expected, but that had definitely not been a false labor contraction. Nope, Little Bit was preparing to come into the world without Ian present. To hell with the curse jar—she'd fill it with money later. "Fuck, fuck, fuck! No, Little Bit, not now. Sweetie, you can't come out until Daddy gets home. Please… oh please."

Once the pain receded, she stood up again and shuffled over to the bed. Grabbing her cell phone, she sat down and quickly found the app to help her time the contractions. Maybe it was false labor—she'd read that the intensity could fluctuate. "Please, please, please, God. Not yet."

Sitting upright against the headboard while using the wedge pillow Ian had gotten her for support, she stretched her swollen legs out on the bed. One hand rubbed her distended belly while the other cupped the bottom of it. The baby didn't feel lower than normal, which meant he or she hadn't dropped into the birth canal yet. Was that a good or bad sign? Angie couldn't remember, and she didn't want to wake Kristen or Harper to ask.

As the seconds on her timer ticked by, the phone rang in her hand, startling her, and she checked the screen.

Incoming call: Ian

She'd made him promise to contact her, no matter what time it was in Tampa, as soon as he could after the raid. She quickly swiped the screen and lifted the device to her ear. "Ian?"

"Yeah, Angel, we got her. Mom and her nurse are okay and—"

The relief she felt at that news tempered her fear that she was going into labor with Ian on the other side of the world. "Oh, thank God! Can I—can I talk to her?"

"She's in the vehicle behind me, but I want you to go back to sleep. I'll have her call you around seven a.m. your time, okay? We're almost at the airport, and we'll take off within the next thirty minutes or so. How are you and Little Bit doing?"

Taking a deep breath, she let it out slowly. "So far so good. I just… I just really need you back here as soon as you can."

"What's wrong? Are you all right?"

"Yeah! Oh, yeah, I'm fine, honey. I miss you, and I guess I'm a little anxious. It's just the hormones. I'm sorry—there's nothing to worry about." He had so much else on his mind and couldn't get back to Tampa any faster than he was already doing, so she omitted the fact she thought she was in labor. She didn't want him to fret about her. If that added another spanking to the ones she'd intentionally and unintentionally racked up these past few weeks, so be it. A Master took care of his sub, but the sub also took care of her Master, and that's what she was doing now.

"You're sure, Angel?"

"I'm sure." Another contraction began to radiate from her back, and she tightened her hold on the phone. She struggled to keep the strain out of her voice. "Give your mom a hug and kiss from me, and tell her I'll talk to her later, okay?"

"I will. We're pulling into the airport. I'll call you in the morning, your time, and see you in about eighteen or nineteen hours. Love you, Angel."

"Love you too, Master." The second she disconnected the call, Angie groaned out loud as the contraction reached its peak. "Shit, shit, shit."

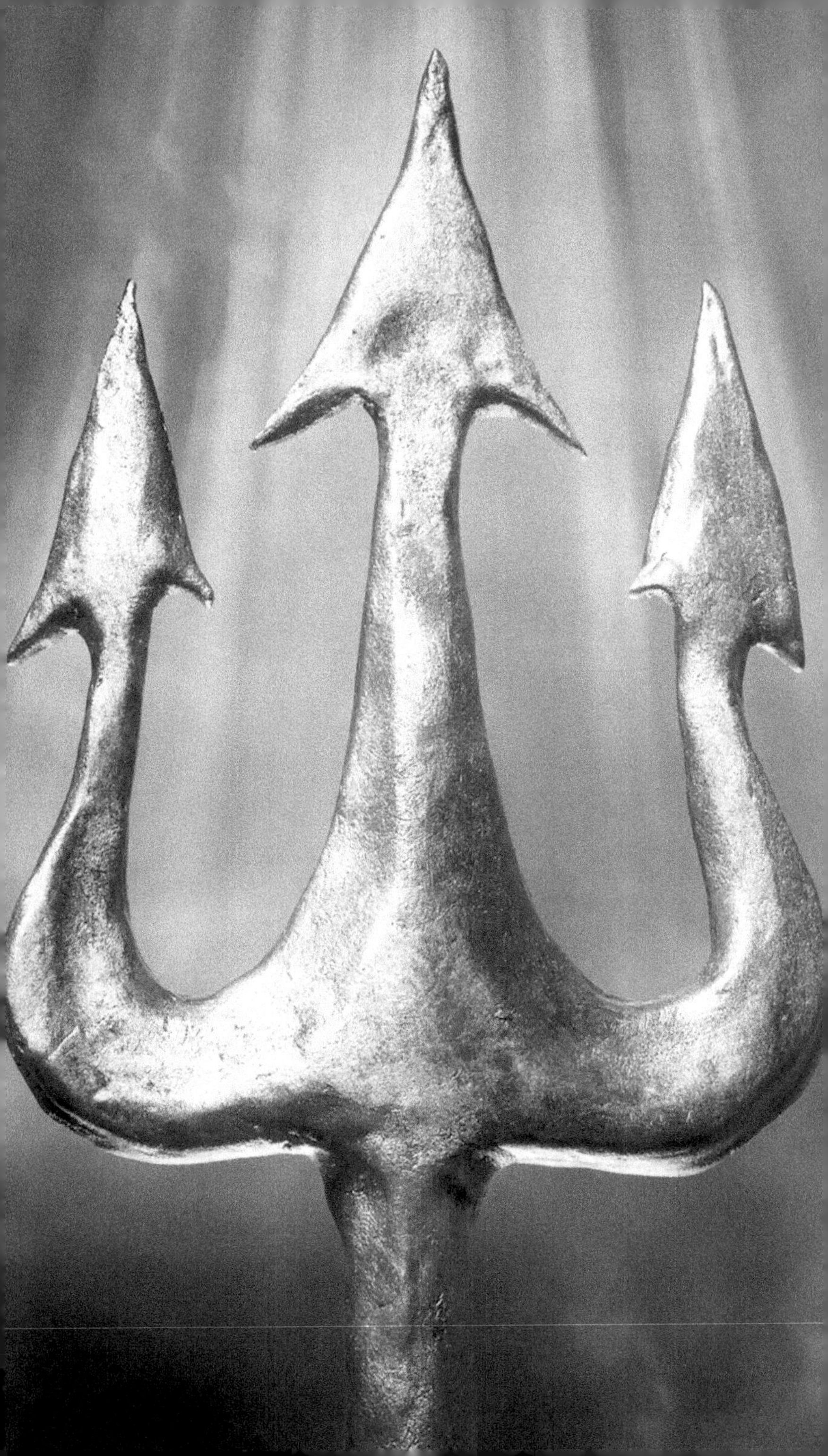

CHAPTER TWELVE

When the call disconnected, Ian pulled the phone from his ear and stared at it.

Nick glanced at his front-seat passenger and noted his frown before returning his gaze to the road before him. "Something wrong?"

Devon was operating the SUV behind them with their mother onboard. All members of Trident's Alpha and Omega teams would be in the air as soon as they were cleared to take off. Carter and Jordyn had Xiao at a secure location, waiting for their MSS contacts to pick him up and return him to China. Nick doubted the man would ever see the inside of a courtroom—odds were, he'd be tortured during an interrogation. After he gave up his secrets, he'd finally be rewarded with a swift death.

Before heading back to Scotland, the Steel Corps team would escort Jocelyn to the clinic to retrieve her things and then put her on the next commercial flight to Manila, where her parents still lived. Although she was still shaken from the entire incident, she was unharmed. Nick wondered if she would stay with Operation Smile after this or find a permanent position in a nice, safe hospital somewhere.

Tucking his phone into one of the thigh pockets of his black BDUs, Ian shook his head. "Angie said no, but…"

"But what?" Nick's eyes widened as he split his attention between his brother and the road. "You don't think she's in labor, do you?" He met Jake's gaze in the rearview mirror. His husband's eyes narrowed in a "shut-up" expression. Yeah, Nick probably should have kept that question to himself. There was nothing Ian could do for Angie from the Philippines, and verbalizing that fact, even in a roundabout way, was going to do nothing but freak him out.

Biting his bottom lip, Ian whipped out his phone again and hit a speed dial button. When the call was answered, he said, "Egghead, get a location on my wife's cell phone." He paused. "Tell me if she's at the compound or at the fucking hospital having my kid, damn it… no, I'm not kidding, asshole. Find out now, or you're a dead man."

A few minutes later, the vehicles pulled into the hangar where Chuck was waiting with the two pilots. The relief Nick saw in his father's eyes when he pulled his wife from the first SUV and into his arms almost brought him to tears. From the back seat, Jake tapped his shoulder. "Let's get the family back to Tampa in time for Little Bit."

Nick glanced around and saw they were the only two still sitting in any of the three vehicles. Everyone else had poured out and quickly transferred all the bags and weapon cases into the jet. He hesitated a moment to wipe his eyes, and Jake squeezed his shoulder in support. "That's going to be us in thirty or forty years—hopefully not on the tail end of a kidnapping, though—but our love will still be going strong, just like theirs."

He met Jake's green eyes in the mirror again. "Think we'll have grandkids by then?"

His husband snorted. "Now, there's a scary thought. I guess that'll be up to our kids if we do or not, but I'd like to think so."

"So do I."

"Come on. Let's get going before Ian starts bitching."

From the relaxed look on his older brother's face when Nick and Jake got out of the vehicle, it was clear Angie was still at the compound. Good, she wasn't in labor yet. Hopefully, she'd stay that way until the jet landed in Tampa.

Thoughts of Jake and him having a child or two occupied Nick's mind as he helped load the gear until well after they'd taken off. Should they adopt or use a surrogate? Either way, they'd have at least a year or so to plan for the arrival. That seemed so far away, and yet it wasn't. Images of Jake holding a baby had Nick smiling to himself. It was probably a good thing they lived right next door to his brothers and sisters-in-law and their growing families because Nick and Jake had a lot to learn about raising a kid.

"What's that smile for?" his mother asked as she took the seat next to him that Jake had just vacated a few minutes before. Nick's father had finally released his wife's hand—he held it for well over an hour as if she'd disappear again if he let go. The couple had sat on one of the jet's couches toward the back of the plane while Nick and Jake relaxed in one of the rows of first-class-style seating toward the front of the cabin.

Grasping Marie's hand, he brought it to his lips and kissed her knuckles. "Just glad to have you back in one piece."

"Nicholas Charles Sawyer, I've been able to read your expressions since you were a toddler. I always knew when you were up to something." She winked before adding, "Like now."

He smirked and shook his head. "I never could hide anything from you. But… for now, I'm not ready to talk about it. Soon, but not yet. There's nothing to worry about—it's a good thing."

She stared at him for a few moments before nodding and smiling. "I can wait, but just remember, I'm not getting any younger."

"Arrrgghhhh! Son of a flying beach ball! Shit, shit, shit!" Angie rode out the contraction as Kristen finally pulled into the hospital's parking lot. Harper and Jenn were back at Angie and Ian's apartment with JD and Mara. When she'd realized the contractions were coming at fourteen-minute intervals, Angie had panicked and called her obstetrician's twenty-four-hour hotline, even though she knew most women didn't go to the hospital until their contractions were around five minutes apart. It hadn't taken long for Dr. Monique Sellares to ascertain that one, Angie was in labor. Two, she was freaking out. And three, she had someone available who could drive her. Monique was a sub at The Covenant, but she was a take-charge woman when she was in doctor mode. She'd assured Angie she'd meet her in the maternity ward and that it was highly doubtful she'd give birth in Kristen's SUV—definitely something Angie didn't want to do.

Her sister-in-law chuckled as she pulled into a parking space near the hospital's main lobby entrance. "Been there, done that. Feel free to curse your head off, Ang. I won't tell. And if Ian demands you fill up the swear jar when he gets here, I'll gladly take a spanking from Devon when I tell your Dom to take a flying leap off a fucking pier." She put the vehicle in park and opened her door. "Sit tight while I get someone with a wheelchair."

"I can walk."

Kristen's eyes narrowed. "No, you can't. Pampering starts now—you'll thank me later. Trust me when I say if you're not in a maternity room by the time the next contraction hits, you'll be thrilled I insisted on the wheelchair."

She let out a sigh as the last of the intense waves of pain eased. "Fine. But hurry—I don't want my water breaking in your car."

Laughing, Kristen climbed out of the driver's seat. "You and me both. That's why I put all those towels under you and on the floor."

When the door shut, Angie leaned her head back and waited, trying to pull herself together and not being very successful. Tears welled up and rolled down her cheeks, and she quickly wiped them away before squeezing her eyelids shut to stem the flow of new ones. "Damn it, Ian. Make CC fly that plane as fast as he can. I don't want to do this alone."

But she wouldn't be alone. Kristen, Harper, and Shelby were all her backup Lamaze coaches. All three had gone through the course and knew what to do. Kristen and Harper did it while expecting their own children, and Shelby had coached a friend of hers whose boyfriend had left her high and dry hours after she told him about the baby.

Angie would never fault Ian for not being here in her time of need, nor would she ever be jealous that his mother had taken precedence for the first time in their marriage—there was no one to blame except whoever had abducted Marie and her nurse. Shit happened, more often than not, when it came to the Trident Security teams and their families. Angie had known that from the start. While it really sucked Ian was somewhere over the Philippine Sea, heading toward the skies above the Pacific Ocean, there was nothing either one of them could do about it but pray Little Bit waited for his or her daddy to get there.

The passenger door opened, and Angie jumped as her eyes flew open to see Kristen holding out her hand. Behind her was a male orderly with a wheel-chair. She might have found him intimidating if she didn't have other things on her mind. He was huge, almost as big as Travis "Tiny" Daultry, the head secu-rity guard of the compound and club. Tiny, a former professional football player, was six-foot-eight and about two-hundred-eighty pounds, most of which was muscle. He was also the biggest mush in the world. JD wasn't old enough yet, but Ian's employee would lie down on the floor for little Mara and let her climb all over him. Angie hoped he found someone special one of these days—she'd love to see him married with children. He'd make a great father.

By the time the next contraction hit, Angie was lying on a bed in one of the labor and delivery rooms and admitting Kristen was right. If she were on foot, she would've ended up on the ground, begging for a wheelchair. A nurse named Ginny, dressed in scrubs with whimsical panda bears all over them, was getting ready to hook Angie up to all sorts of monitors and an IV port. "Just breathe through the pain."

Angie almost punched her.

Obviously used to death glares, the nurse waited until the contraction was gone, then helped Angie change into an ugly hospital gown. A fetal monitor was attached to Angie's swollen belly, and after a few moments of listening to the *beep-beep-beep*, Ginny announced Little Bit was doing just fine. Fifteen minutes later, Angie's last contraction had been assessed via another monitor, an ultrasound had been done to see if there had been any significant loss of amniotic fluid, and Ginny had checked for dilation. At only two centimeters, she had a ways to go, but she was still afraid Ian wouldn't make it on time.

Kristen came in with a large cup of coffee she'd found somewhere for herself and a plastic pitcher filled with ice chips for Angie. The woman had been a godsend since the moment Angie had called her to say she was in labor. She'd quickly taken charge, and after leaving instructions about JD with Jenn, she'd grabbed the go-baby-bag, as Ian had called it, and gotten Angie to the hospital. Once upstairs in the Labor & Delivery ward, she'd double-checked Angie's admission paperwork that'd been filled out in advance and unpacked a few things, putting everything in an orderly fashion on a bedside tray table within Angie's reach. Then, before she'd stepped out to find the pantry available to patients and their coaches, Kristen had turned the room's television on, finding reruns of *Friends* on one of the channels.

As she sat in a comfortable chair in the labor room, Kristen's phone chimed, and she swiped the screen to answer it. "Hey, Jenn. We're all settled in. She's not dilated much, so it'll probably be a while. How's JD?" Whatever the answer had been, Kristen smiled. "Great. Now, get some sleep. I'll call if anything happens, but I think that'll be way after the sun comes up… I will. Bye."

She disconnected the call and blew Angie two kisses. "Those are from Jenn and Harper. JD went right back to sleep after his bottle and a new diaper. Mara didn't wake up at all." Since the little girl slept through the brief chaos after Angie roused Harper and then called Kristen and Jenn, it'd been easier for them to bring JD downstairs instead of carrying Mara up to Kristen's apartment. Harper had a court hearing first thing in the morning for a few hours, so Jenn would babysit both kids.

Reaching into her huge purse, Kristen pulled out her iPad. "I think you better call Ian and let him know." Before Angie could protest, she held up a hand. "I know there's nothing he can do from thousands of feet in the air, but if your husband is anything like mine, and I know he is, then he's going to be mad if you wait." She held up the device. "I brought this and the charger so you can Skype with him for hours. If Little Bit refuses to wait, then I'll record the birth for you. This way, even if it's over the airwaves, Ian will be here with you."

Angie smiled, knowing Kristen was right. "You know, you're my favorite sister-in-law."

"I'm your only sister-in-law, and I love you too. Now let me call Devon and tell him to get you and Ian patched into each other."

She nodded, then bit her bottom lip as another contraction hit.

CHAPTER THIRTEEN

"Whattaya mean she's in labor?" Ian knew that was a stupid question to ask Devon, who was on the jet's phone with Kristen, but he couldn't think of anything else to say. Apparently, he hadn't kept his voice down because everyone in the cabin was now awake and staring at him. It wasn't supposed to happen that way—he should be by Angie's side every second until after Little Bit came into the world. He'd promised her he'd be there. While she'd understood his need to fly twenty hours away to the Philippines, it still didn't make him feel any less guilty. He'd been torn between the two women who meant the most to him in the entire universe. One's life had been in danger, while the other was bringing a new life—his child—into the world.

He jumped to his feet and began searching for

where he'd left his cell phone in the area designed to look like a living room behind several rows of first-class-style seats. It even had a built-in bar, and right now, he could use a stiff drink. "Shit, where the hell is my phone?"

"It's in your thigh pocket," Devon responded, "but don't call her. She's having a contraction. And calm down. She hasn't been in labor for long. They're at the hospital, and everything's fine. Kristen says it's going to be at least several hours—Angie's barely dilated. Egghead, patch him into Kristen's Skype. She has her iPad, and this way, he can see Angie while he talks to her. That should keep him from punching a hole in the ceiling and sending us crashing into the ocean."

Thrusting his hands into his hair, Ian glared at Devon as he started to pace. The wise-ass shouldn't throw stones in a glass house. He'd freaked out much worse than Ian was now when Kristen had gone into labor with JD since that'd finally happened after several false alarms. But this was the real thing with Angie. They wouldn't have admitted her if it wasn't, right? "This can't be fucking happening!"

After pivoting once more to go back in the other direction, he stopped short when he came face to face with his mother. She patted his chest. "She's going to be fine—she's a strong woman, and the female sex has been doing this since the beginning of time."

"I know." *She has to be okay.* "How… how long

before…" A lump formed in his throat, and he swallowed hard. "I wanted to be there, but there's no way we'll—"

"Ian, stop. It could be a few hours, or it could be much longer. I was in labor with you for twenty-seven hours."

"What?" His mouth gaped as he stared at her in disbelief. How had he not known that? "Seriously?"

She chuckled. "Yes, seriously. Your father was such a basket case, they almost had to sedate him."

"She's making that up," Chuck retorted, but the smile on his face belied his statement. "All right, maybe I was a little nuts, but that was because you, boy, weren't easy on your mother. At least Devon, John, and Nick were much faster. Nick was the longest labor next to you, and he was out within six hours."

"That's because he weighed the most out of all of you and the fact I hadn't been pregnant in years." Nick had been a surprise pregnancy nine years after John had been born since their parents had thought they were done having children.

"Hey, Boss-man, I've got Ang on Skype."

After giving his mother a swift kiss on the cheek, Ian hurried over and took the laptop and seat Brody offered him. In his rush, he fumbled the computer. Brody snatched it before it hit the floor and handed it back to him. "Chill and channel your inner Dom— she doesn't need to see you freaking out."

Knowing his friend was right—Ian had to be calm

and strong for Angie—he took a few deep breaths. A pair of noise-canceling headphones had been plugged into the laptop, and he put them on to drown out the jet's white noise and the few conversations taking place. The video feed bounced around while he waited for Angie to come into view. Kristen's voice filtered through. "Hang on a sec, Ian."

Finally, his wife was there, looking more beautiful than ever but a bit upset. Her eyes were red, and her face had a sheen of perspiration. Her long, blonde hair was up in the ponytail he loved to tug on when they were scening. "Hey, Angel, can you hear me?"

"Ian, I'm sorry—"

Her sob and sudden tears almost ripped him to shreds. "Hush. There's nothing to be sorry about. You can't control Mother Nature—trust me, I've tried on many occasions." *Just not in terms of procreation.* "If Little Bit decides to come into the world before I get there, then I'm going to stay with you on here for the entire time and watch and coach you as best I can, okay?"

The video tilted a little as she wiped her eyes with a tissue. "Okay."

"So, give me a sit-rep. Is Monique there yet?" *She better be.*

Angie shook her head. "Not yet, but she'll be here in a little while. The nurse told her I'd be in labor for hours, so she's getting some more sleep, but she said to call her if I started to progress. I'm only two centimeters dilated, and the baby's heart rate is good. The contractions are still about fourteen minutes apart."

"What do they feel like?" He wanted to know everything she was experiencing. The wonder of giving birth was the most special gift God had given women—men couldn't handle it. Of that, Ian was certain after watching Angie's body change and react over the past nine months as Little Bit grew inside her. Give Ian and his teams a mission, and they had it covered. Make one of them push something the size of a peanut out of their cocks? Yeah, they'd scream and beg for morphine. Make it the size of an orange, and C-sections would've been performed for every delivery since ancient times. And, God forbid, they had to give birth to a baby the size of a watermelon, like Angie would do soon, because the human race would've been extinct not long after it was created.

"In terms you can relate to? Right now, it feels like my nipples were moved to my lower back and you just took off a set of clamps." He chuckled at her analogy. "Trust me, I'll let you know when the urge to castrate you hits. And I'm warning you now, do not even *think* of tallying up my curse words for future punishments or money for the swear jar because I have a feeling I'm in for pain like I've never felt before."

"I wish I could take the pain from you, Angel. Don't worry about cursing—hell, you can curse *me* if you need to—you get a free pass for the next few days. I love you."

"I love you too." She paused. "Is your mom awake? Is she up to talking? I'd like to say hi before the next contraction."

"Yeah, she just sat down next to me. Hang on." Removing the headphones, he gave them to his mother and turned the laptop, so she could see Angie. "Talk normal—she'll hear you."

Once she had the headphones on, Marie waved at the laptop's camera. "Hi, sweetie. How are you? I'm so sorry Ian's not there, but thanks to technology, it's almost like he's there."

He put his arm around his mother as the two women chatted for a moment. Having lost her own parents in her early twenties, Angie had developed a close bond with Chuck and Marie over the past few years, and they often talked on the phone. On more than one occasion, Angie had mentioned she'd gotten lucky in the in-law department and loved it when his parents visited.

His mother tapped his leg. "Tell Nick, Jake, Devon, and your dad to come here a minute, please. Chuck and I have something we want to tell all of you."

Ian's eyes narrowed, but he did as he was told. Once the four men joined them, Marie looked back at the screen. She still had the headphones on. "We were going to announce this when we got home but might as well do it now. Dad and I are going to semi-retire over the next few months." Ian's eyebrows weren't the only ones to shoot upward. "We've been talking about this for a year or so now and think it's time. Chuck has a good executive board in place, and I'll continue with my charity work only. I've already advised my partners that I'm leaving the practice. And… we'll be moving to Tampa or Clearwater by the end of the year. Our whole family is in Florida, and at our age, that's where we want to be—with our family. If that's okay with all of you, of course."

"Of course!" The sentiment was unanimous among her sons and son-in-law, and as far as Ian could tell, Angie had agreed as well.

Ian reached out and shook his father's hand. "It's about damn time, Dad. When are you getting the fishing boat you've been talking about forever?"

A wink preceded Chuck's response. "It's already in the works. And I already have one of my top agents looking for an apartment or townhouse for us. We don't need a huge house anymore."

"Whoops," Marie declared, taking off the head-phones. "Hang on, sweetie. I'm giving you back to Ian so you can curse the day he was born to him."

"WHAT DO YOU MEAN THE LABOR STALLED?" ANGIE asked Monique at the same time Ian did via Skype. She'd been having contractions every thirteen or four-teen minutes for several hours, but now they were coming about twenty-five minutes apart and not as strong. The nurse had contacted her obstetrician, and she'd come to the hospital immediately. "What—is that bad for the baby?"

"No, it's not. Here, let me take that from you for a minute." Monique gently pulled the iPad from Angie's shaky grasp and sat with one hip on the bed next to her, turning the device so Ian could see both of them. "A stalled labor is not uncommon, and there's nothing to worry about. I believe the reason your contractions have slowed down is due to emotional stress, so I want you to try to relax a bit. Get comfy and take a nap if you can. There's a full bathroom across the hallway where you can take a shower if you want. I also recommend you walk the halls when you feel up to it. All these things can help get the labor progressing again. Ian, talk about memories you share, tell some jokes, or be your usual, sarcastic self, anything to make Angie smile and relax. Talk her into subspace if you can. As a last resort, Angie, I can give you a sedative that won't harm the baby, or I can start you on Pitocin."

"No! No Pitocin." That was one of the things she'd learned about in an online chatroom for mothers and mothers-to-be. The drug was supposed to induce labor, but it could also result in needing a C-section. Also, if she had any chance of not giving birth until Ian arrived, induction would probably cancel that out.

Monique patted her hand. "I remember you telling me you didn't want to go that route, if at all possible, but I'm just reminding you it's an option. The baby is not in any distress. Do those things I suggested, and we'll keep monitoring you and the baby. As long as you're both okay, we'll let nature take its course. When he or she is ready, it'll happen, okay?"

Taking a deep breath, Angie let it out slowly. "Okay." Suddenly, the lack of sleep made her tired, and she yawned. "Maybe I should try to nap."

"That sounds like a good idea, Angel." Ian's voice had softened now that he knew she and the baby were all right. "Did Kristen bring earbuds for the iPad?"

"I have an extra set in the go-bag in the closet. Why?"

"Ask Kristen to get them for you and put them in. I want to talk to you without anyone else hearing me."

Within a few minutes, Angie and Ian were alone together, although they were still thousands of miles apart. Monique had left to see another patient, while Kristen had gone downstairs to get some breakfast with Shelby and Tori, who'd arrived to see how things were going. Before leaving, Kristen had turned off most of the room's lights and closed the door.

"Are you comfortable, Angel?"

"As comfy as I can get, I guess." It had taken a few moments to get the adjustable bed and her big belly into positions she could sleep in. She was on her left side, with only the right earbud in so she could hear him. He was standing in the jet's galley, where he'd gone for some privacy. As he'd instructed, she'd folded open the cover to the iPad so it stood on its side on the tray table, facing her. Kristen had plugged it into an outlet to charge it up again after the battery had run down for the second time since they'd started Skyping.

"Good girl. I want you to just relax and listen to my voice. Close your eyes."

"Mm-kay."

"We're in the garden at the club. The Doms and subs are all watching. You're naked, my little exhibitionist." She smiled as his sexy, deep voice warmed her skin. "Everyone is admiring your beauty as I lead you to the St. Andrew's cross. You stand face first against the soft leather and spread your legs for me. I run my hands up your sides to your arms and lift them, outstretched above your head. I can smell your arousal, Angel. It's the most intoxicating scent in the world to me. You beg me to touch you there, but you know there's no topping from the bottom. It'll earn you a punishment, but you love my punishments—at least, when I finally let you come, you do."

"You do get very creative, Sir." Falling into D/s mode was instantaneous when he spoke to her like this. She didn't even have to think about it. Her body just reacted of its own accord. All she had to do was just feel.

"That's my good subbie." She could hear the

smile in his voice. "I strap your wrists to the cross, then kiss my way down your spine to your luscious ass as I drop to my knees. I inhale deeply because your scent is so much stronger now. I drag my hands down one leg, leaving goosebumps in their wake. Then I strap your ankle to the cross and do the same to your other leg. I check each restraint, making sure they aren't too tight. Your body, mind, and soul are safe with me, Angel."

Her skin was tingling. Ian loved touching her bare flesh as much as she loved letting him.

"You're now at my mercy—but you were before I restrained you, weren't you, my love?"

"Yes, Sir." Her words came out as a murmur as the edges of subspace teased her mind.

"What shall I do with you?"

"Anything you want, Master."

Ian chuckled. "That's right—I'll do anything I want, and you'll beg for more. You know how I love when you scream my name when I let you come. Give me a color, Angel."

Even though he was obviously not doing anything but talking to her, they were still sceneing, and that meant rules were followed. "Green, Sir. I'm—actually, I'm not, Sir. A contraction is coming."

"That's okay. Ride it out. Is this one stronger than before?"

"Uh-uh." But it still hurt. She did her Lamaze breathing until the pain began to fade. Opening her eyes, she looked at the screen. While he was trying to be strong for her, she could see the worry and guilt for not being there on his face. "Sorry, Sir."

"Okay, new rule until Little Bit gets here—no apologizing, Angel. I'm in awe of you. You're stronger than you know, and I'm so proud of you."

She sniffled, fighting back her tears, exhaustion beginning to overtake her. Her eyes fluttered shut. "I love you, Ian."

"I love you too, Angel. Go to sleep. I'll be right here watching over you."

CHAPTER FOURTEEN

Before Devon's vehicle came to a complete stop, Ian already had the passenger door open and was climbing out. Leaving his brother and Brody's laptop behind, he hightailed it into the hospital's lobby and didn't bother stopping at the front desk. When a gray-haired guard called out to him, Ian just yelled over his shoulder, "My wife's in labor."

"Good luck!" Guess it wasn't the first time a frantic father-to-be had rushed past the older man.

Bypassing the elevator, Ian shoved open the door to the stairs and then took them two at a time up to the third floor. He remembered where the Labor & Delivery ward was from the tour they'd taken about three weeks ago as part of their Lamaze class. Angie's contractions were now three minutes apart, and she was almost fully dilated. Somehow, some way, Little Bit had waited for him to get there. Angie had been in labor for over eighteen hours, and it didn't look like she'd make it to nineteen.

During the long, gut-wrenching flight, CC had managed to catch a few jet streams, saving them about thirty minutes of airtime, which looked like it had made a world of difference in getting Ian to the hospital in time for the delivery. After landing, Ian had been chomping at the bit while they'd taxied to Trident's assigned hangar. The second the stairs had hit the ground, he'd been running down them. Thankfully, Devon had his head on straighter than his older brother because out of the two of them, he was the only one who had his car keys in hand—Ian had forgotten his set in his go-bag, which was still on the jet. His parents would catch a ride with the teams, all of whom were headed to the hospital to wait for the newest arrival to the Trident family.

Bursting out into the hallway, he almost ran over a nurse. "Sorry! Wife's in labor!"

"Good luck!"

He ran down the hall, through the doors under the L&D sign, and slid to a stop at the reception desk. "My wife, Angelina Sawyer. Labor. What room?"

Before the startled woman could answer him, he heard, "Ian! In here!"

Shelby waved to him from one of the rooms. She was wearing scrubs and holding another set. "Hurry! She had to start pushing."

Holy shit!

Rushing into the room, he tried to make sense of the chaos. Angie's legs were up in stirrups, with a blue sheet covering them. She was screaming, cursing, sweating, and panting all at the same time. Her gaze latched onto his, and he couldn't miss the relief he saw in her eyes.

Kristen was by her side, holding her hand and counting out loud. "Eight... nine... ten. There you go, relax."

"Uuuuugh!" Angie collapsed back on the incline of the bed. Her face was beet red as she tried to catch her breath. "Ian! You... made it!"

Several nurses were going about their duties as Monique pulled a stool over to sit on and got ready to deliver the baby. "Just in time, Ian. Throw those scrubs on over your clothes and wash your hands and arms. We probably only have another few contractions to go, so hurry."

He must have frozen in place because Shelby grabbed his arm. "Come here—these are your size." She led him to the sink and turned on the water. In under a minute, he'd soaped up, rinsed off, and managed to get the scrub shirt and pants over his T-shirt and BDUs. Shelby squatted down in front of him with two shoe covers. "Let me put these on over your boots so you don't have to scrub again."

Damn it. He hadn't even realized he still had his dirty boots on. Thankfully, they were dry, and he hoped Angie and the hospital staff didn't notice the brownish stains of blood against the worn, black leather.

Once he was set, Kristen stepped away from Angie's side and let him move in before giving him a kiss on the cheek. "We'll wait outside with everyone else. I'm glad you made it."

He didn't have time to thank Kristen or Shelby because Angie grabbed his hand and squeezed like she was trying to crush his metacarpals. She screamed as the contraction took hold.

"Dad, count to ten for her," one of the nurses prodded.

"Huh?" *Oh, right, Lamaze. Counting. Got it.* "Um, one, two, three..."

Once more, Angie collapsed at number ten. She shook her head on the pillow behind it. "I... I can't do this, Ian! The epidural's not helping. Please, I can't!"

Leaning down, he kissed her forehead, then whispered in her ear. "Yes, you can, Angel. Do you know how I know?"

"N-no."

"Because you, my beautiful wife, are the strongest woman I've ever met, and I know quite a few. You have to be strong to put up with me. Every time life knocked you down, you got up again. You're going to be the best mother in the world. And because of you, I'm going to try to be the best father I can possibly be. We'll probably stumble a few times, and we may even fall, but we'll get up again and make sure Little Bit and any other children we may have will be prepared to take the world by storm when it's their time. So whattaya say? Are you ready to have this baby?"

"Well, when you put it that way..."

He brushed her damp hair from her face, which started to fill with pain once more. She struggled to sit up. Putting his arm around her back, he helped her as she got ready to push. "I've got you, Angel. Let's do this."

———

With her head resting on Chuck's shoulder, Marie surveyed the maternity ward's waiting room. It was filled with her sons' friends, employees, and teammates as they all awaited Little Bit's arrival. The operatives had come straight from the airport, while others had already been there. When Kristen had come out not long ago, after passing the coaching torch to Ian, she'd announced it wouldn't be much longer, and now everyone was even more excited than they'd been.

It didn't matter what the baby's gender was, as long as he or she was healthy, but after having four boys herself, Marie was looking forward to spoiling a little girl. God help her, though, when she was old enough to date because Ian would be cleaning his guns every time a young man picked her up—then again, Ian's daughter would probably be sitting right next to him, cleaning her own guns.

"Mom?"

She looked up and smiled at Devon and JD. Her grandson was the spitting image of his father at that age, and it brought back a rush of memories for her. When Chuck had taken Ian to meet his baby brother for the first time at the hospital, he'd asked the two-and-a-half-year-old if he knew which one of the newborns in their bassinets on the other side of the window was Devon. Without hesitation, Ian pointed at the correct infant. "Dat's my baby brudder!" He'd paused and then announced, "I'm gonna be the best big brudder in the *whole* world, Daddy."

And he had been and still was. When their time came to depart this life, Chuck and Marie knew their growing family's new patriarch would take care of them until his own dying day.

"Want to hold him for a bit?" Devon asked.

She held out her hands. "That's a silly question—of course I do."

Gently taking her grandson, she cuddled him close as Devon squatted in front of her. Marie stared down at the eyes that matched her own and those of all her sons. Unexpected tears rolled down her cheek, and Devon reached up and wiped some away. "Hey, it's okay, Mom. You're here, and you will be for a long time."

If things had turned out differently, her family might have been mourning right then despite the birth of Little Bit. She thanked God that wasn't the case. She owed her sons her life, and wasn't that ironic? They may not be perfect, but then again, who was? However, she would forever be proud of the men they'd become. They were good husbands to their spouses and would be excellent fathers to any children they had. After all, they'd had the best role model around in that department.

Chuck's arm had been resting behind her neck, and he squeezed her shoulder. "Darn right, you'll be. And there will be plenty more grandkids for you to dote on before you know it."

Sniffling, she raised her gaze, and it settled on Nick and Jake, sitting next to each other on the opposite side of the room. Their heads were close together, and they were deep in a private conversation. Her smile appeared again and grew as she turned back to her husband. "I think you're right."

"Break out the cigars!" Ian declared from the doorway, with sparkling eyes and the broadest grin Marie had ever seen on his face. "It's a girl! God help me and any little shit who wants to date her someday."

Everyone jumped to their feet, cheered, and gathered around.

"What's her name?" Kristen prodded since the new parents had kept a list of all possible names for boys and girls to themselves.

"Peyton Marie Sawyer weighs eight pounds five ounces, has a full head of black hair, and came kicking and screaming into the world, just as I knew she would." He accepted a fat cigar with a baby-pink ribbon around it from Brody as Nick and Boomer handed others out. Apparently, they'd stocked up on them in both pink and blue for the occasion.

Stepping over to his parents, Ian shook his father's hand, smiled down at JD, and then kissed Marie on the cheek. "She's beautiful, just like her mother and grandmother, and you have permission to spoil her rotten—although you were probably planning on doing that anyway."

"You know me too well, sweetheart," Marie responded. "I'm so happy for you. How's Angie?"

"Exhausted but happy." Turning to face the rest of his family and friends, he said, "Nick, since Dev was my best man, Angie and I would like you to be Peyton's godfather."

His youngest brother's eyes and smile widened. "Me? Absolutely! I'm honored, bro, and I won't let you down."

"Good, and I know you won't. And that leaves just one last announcement." His eyes watered as his gaze fell on Jenn, and his voice grew thick. "Baby-girl, I remember standing in a similar maternity waiting room over twenty-two years ago when your dad came in and announced you were a girl. I think I fell in love with you at that exact moment, and I hadn't even seen you yet. When Jeff asked me to be your godfather, I honestly didn't fully understand what it meant when I said yes. But now I do, and I've never regretted it. It has been my honor and privilege to serve as godparent to such a beautiful and exceptional young woman, and I'm thrilled to pass the title on. Angie and I would like nothing more than for you to be Peyton's godmother."

There wasn't a dry eye in the room as Jenn rushed forward, clearly too overcome for words, and threw her arms around Ian's neck. He held her tightly for a few moments until she regained some of her composure. Through her sniffles, she finally answered him. "Yes, Uncle Ian. I'll be there for her every step of the way, just like you were there for me. Thank you for the honor."

"You're welcome, Jenn. Always know I'm proud of you." With a final squeeze, he released her, and they both wiped away some more tears. Then Ian hitched a thumb over his shoulder. "I've got to get back to Angie. Thanks for being here, everyone. The nurse said you'll all be able to see Peyton in about fifteen minutes through the nursery window, although I'm not sure they realize how many people are here waiting to see her."

After shaking a few hands again and getting his back slapped a bunch of times, Ian turned toward the door, but a small voice ringing out stopped him in his tracks.

"What-waffle, Unc-en!"

The roomful of people burst out laughing as, with

a huge grin, little Mara repeated herself even louder from her father's arms. "What-waffle, Unc-en!"

Ian just groaned and shook his head. "I'm doomed."

If you're following the best reading order of the Trident Security series and its spinoffs, up next is *Knot a Chance: Doms of The Covenant Book 3*.

For the best reading order of the Trident Security series and its spinoffs, check out the printable list on my website - www.samanthacolebooks.-com/pages/best-reading-order.

Want to know what's coming next? Join my Facebook Group -
Samantha Cole's Sexy Six-Pack's Sirens…

Or sign up for my newsletter -
samanthacolebooks.com/mailing-list

**Knot a Chance: Doms of The Covenant
Book 3**

"Red."

Stefan Lundquist's hand froze at the whispered word. The pen he was holding was an inch away from the contract he'd been about to sign, renewing his Dominant/submissive relationship with Cassandra Myers for another month. His brow furrowed as he was unsure he'd heard her correctly. "What did you say, Cassie?"

There was a long moment of silence as they sat across from each other at his dining room table. Stefan had invited her over to sign the contract, have some dinner, then play for a while, and she'd arrived only a few minutes ago. After the contract was out of the way and they'd eaten, he'd planned on trying a new Shibari design on the beautiful submissive's naked body before burying himself deep inside her. But if she'd said what he thought she'd just said, then none of that was going to happen. He darkened his tone. "I expect an answer, Cassandra. Look at me and repeat yourself."

The twenty-nine-year-old blonde swallowed hard before her eyelids lifted and her gaze met his. Stefan's gut clenched when he saw her hazel eyes were filled with unshed tears. Cassandra's voice was barely any louder when she spoke again. "I said, 'red,' Sir."

Stefan had no idea what was going on. They'd been in a D/s relationship for ten months now. On the ninth of each month, they'd sat down and discussed any changes either wanted to make on their contract before signing it for another four weeks. He'd thought tonight would be no different, but Cassandra obviously didn't agree.

Dropping the pen atop the papers in front of him, he leaned back in his chair, crossed his arms, and stared at the sub. She was what Stefan's father would call "a stunner." Her long, blonde locks fell just below her shoulder blades, and he had to put them in a ponytail before he tied her up when they played, so they were out of his way. A smattering of freckles dusted her nose and cheeks. Her bow-shaped lips were made to be kissed, and there were moments in the past when he'd completely lost track of time while exploring her mouth with his own. The neckline of her shirt was wide and curved, exposing the porcelain skin of her shoulders and neck. As for the rest of her body, the woman had curves that gave most men whiplash as she sashayed past them. At five feet five, she was eight inches shorter than him, unless she was wearing one of the several pairs of fuck-me heels she owned. Stefan loved when she wore them with nothing else on but his collar and ropes. Unfortunately, it appeared he wouldn't be seeing her dressed like that in the future.

"Why are you saying your safeword, little pixie? And, please, speak up."

She cleared her throat and straightened her back. Her voice was stronger this time but still worrisome. "I-I'm sorry, Sir, but I don't want to renew our contract this month." Her lip trembled, and Stefan tried to figure out why. Was she scared of what he was going to do or say? He'd never given her a reason to be afraid of him. Was she nervous for some other reason? Or was she about to lie to him? "I-I've had a lot of fun these past few months, but—but I'd rather not be collared by you or anyone else for a while, Sir."

Her gaze dropped to the table, and Stefan ground his teeth together, trying to keep his frustration in check. *Damn it.* Things had been going great with her. She was the most responsive sub he'd had in a long time when it came to Shibari. She loved being wrapped in his rope designs. The less she could move, the more explosive her orgasms when he finally allowed her to come. What had changed? They'd both gone into the relationship with a clear understanding. Each contract lasted exactly one month. They played either in his townhouse or at The Covenant, the elite **BDSM** club in Tampa they both belonged to. Cassandra waitressed there three evenings a week, four hours per shift, earning her a dramatic reduction on her membership fees in addition to tips. He knew that after living expenses, there wasn't much left over in her pay from her full-time career as a cardiac rehabilitation technician, so the extra job helped her financially and gave her access to the club.

"Cassie, eyes on me." An experienced sub, her response to his command was instantaneous. "You're my submissive until midnight tonight. Until I give you leave, you *will* follow protocol. Now, why don't you want to be collared anymore?"

She took a deep breath and let it out slowly, but her gaze stayed on his. "I've decided to go back to school, Sir, for nursing, and I won't have time for anything else between classes and work."

Okay, this wasn't as bad as he'd thought it was. As her Dom, he could help her. Stefan had recently been promoted to the rank of lieutenant commander in the Coast Guard. While military pay wasn't the greatest, the truth was, he didn't need it. His family came from old money, and a trust fund, which he rarely touched, had been set up for him by his grandfather shortly after Stefan had been born. None of his friends or fellow club members knew about his family's wealth, except The Covenant's three owners, Ian and Devon Sawyer, and their cousin Mitch. Their security guru, Brody Evans, also knew, since he'd done the extensive background check on Stefan during the application process. All members and employees of The Covenant were completely vetted to help maintain privacy and safety, so any skeletons in an applicant's closet were sure to be found.

Despite his family's money, Stefan had been drawn to the military from a young age, although he couldn't recall what had originally set him on the path to enlisting. It was just something he'd always wanted to do. While his family had tried to encourage him to attend law school, like his older sister, Elin, Stefan had signed up for the Coast Guard following his college education, which allowed him to enlist as an officer. Years vacationing in Martha's Vineyard had given him his love for the ocean, and the USCG had given him a better chance of serving on a ship or in a port while remaining in the US. At the time, that'd been important to him. Stefan had always been close to his maternal grandparents, and his greatest fear had been not being stationed near enough to get to them quickly if something had happened to either of them. His grandmother had passed away nine years ago, but he'd been stationed in New Jersey and able to get to the hospital in time to say goodbye to her. Unfortunately, without any warning, his grandfather had died of a heart attack four years later. While Stefan hadn't seen him before he passed, he'd been able to attend the funeral without the huge hassle of traveling from somewhere on the other side of the world.

Stefan ran a hand over his salt-and-pepper crewcut. Like his father before him, he'd started going gray five years ago at the age of thirty-three. He didn't mind, though, because if he let his hair grow out, it was still thick and didn't recede at all. Quite a few friends from high school had already gone partially or completely bald, and he was glad he wasn't one of them. Not that he was vain. He just knew what he looked like completely bald after he and most of the men at The Covenant had shaved their heads in support of a pretty sub named Shelby when she'd been going through chemo. Thankfully, she'd beaten her cancer, but it'd been pretty funny to see all those polished heads before everyone's hair had started growing back.

Sighing, he pushed away all thoughts that didn't have to do with the current situation. To make certain they were both on the same page, he repeated some of Cassandra's words back to her. "So, between school and working at both the hospital and The Covenant, you won't have time to relax and play?"

"No, Sir."

While studying her face, he got the impression she wanted to bolt. He'd never seen her this nervous before and tried to soften his expression and tone of voice. "What if I took care of your membership fees? Then you'd be able to give up your job at The Covenant. Once you get your class schedule, we can plan playtime around it."

Her eyes had gone wide at his offer, but she'd started shaking her head before he'd finished speaking. "No—No, Sir. I-I can't let you do that. I'm sorry, but I think it's best that you take your collar back. There are plenty of unattached subs at the club. Several of them have already expressed interest in taking my place."

Stefan frowned. "You discussed this with the other subs before coming here tonight? Before telling me you want to be uncollared?" Hell, no, he was not happy about that. He should have been the first person to know she was going to use her safeword and return his collar, not the last. "You know better than that, subbie. Your discussing any part of our contract, or the termination of it, with anyone else is not acceptable."

"I'm s-sorry, Sir." Her tears welled up again. "I-I just thought it would be easier if I had a replacement ready for you—you need a sub for your Shibari classes."

That was true. In a few weeks, Stefan was set to begin teaching another course at the club in the fine art of tying a submissive up in designs made from yards of silky rope. When his maternal grandfather had taught Stefan how to create dozens of different types of knots when he was a boy, never had he thought he'd be using the knowledge to decorate naked women with intricate patterns that would put them in subspace.

But Stefan didn't want a new sub—he wanted Cassandra. He'd gotten used to her, and they'd fallen into a comfortable relationship—superficial as it was. He'd made it clear, when they'd done their initial negotiations all those months ago, they were a Dom and his sub—nothing more. Stefan didn't want a girl-friend or slave. He'd gone both those routes before—several times—and none had worked out, which was why he avoided those types of relationships now. Less drama that way.

Damn it, he wasn't ready to give Cassandra up yet. But he didn't have a choice. She'd said her safe-word, and as a respectable Dom, he had to abide by it. That didn't mean he couldn't try to get her to change her mind. "We have a few hours left on the current contract. Do you still want to play tonight?"

When she hesitated and bit her bottom lip, his heart sank. He knew without a doubt what her next words were going to be. "No, Sir, I'd rather not. I'm sorry—I know you didn't expect this tonight, but I-I really should be going."

He had half a mind to ask where she was going in

such a hurry but managed to keep the question in his throat. He didn't want her to know how disappointed he was that she'd ended their time together. Instead, he stood and rounded the table to stand behind her.

"Lift your hair," he commanded. When she obeyed him, his fingers went to her nape, but then he couldn't help himself. Before he unclasped the simple collar he'd given her months ago, he skimmed her bare neck and shoulder with his knuckles, memorizing how soft she was. A shiver flowed through her, and goose bumps appeared across her skin. Damn, he was going to miss her. Taking a deep breath, he undid the clasp and removed the black leather and silver collar from her neck before stuffing it into the front pocket of his navy-blue Dockers. He wanted nothing more than to bend down and kiss his way across her shoulder to her neck and then nuzzle her ear. But if he did that, he'd be left standing there with a hard-on when she walked out the door.

Taking a step to the side, he held out his hand. When she took it, he helped her to her feet, then kissed the back of her hand. "It was an honor to be your Dom, Cassie. I wish you all the best." He couldn't resist adding, "As for my offer—paying your membership while you're in school—I'd like you to agree to it, no strings attached. This way you only have to work one job and can better concentrate on your studies." When it looked like she was going to turn him down again, he squeezed her hand. "Please accept my gift. It would mean a lot to me."

She sucked her bottom lip between her teeth. Seconds ticked by as she held his brown-eyed gaze before nodding. "If it means that much to you, Sir, thank you."

He knew the smile on his face didn't reach his eyes, but he tried to keep the tone of his voice light. "No, thank *you*, Cassie. It's my pleasure. Maybe it'll give us the opportunity to play on occasion."

It didn't escape his notice that she winced slightly at his hopeful statement. He wanted to ask her about it but thought it was best not to. He'd find out soon but not tonight. She was too upset, and he got the feeling she'd shut down further if he interrogated her. He'd figured out months ago the best way to get Cassandra to open up was to tie her down. And that clearly wasn't going to happen right now. "I'll talk to Master Mitch tomorrow and make the arrangements. He'll probably need two-weeks' notice."

"That's fine, Sir. Classes start next Wednesday, so they'll only overlap with my club shift for a few days—I've already made arrangements for two of my shifts to be covered by other waitresses." When he didn't release her hand, she glanced down to where they were joined. "I-I really should go."

With great reluctance, Stefan let her go then escorted her to the front door, where he fought the urge to kiss her. "Goodbye, little pixie."

"Goodbye, Sir."

Ten minutes after she walked out of his life, Stefan sat on his living room couch with an almost-empty glass of scotch—one that had been filled for the second time moments before. He stared at the coiled lengths of rope he'd set out on the coffee table earlier in the evening. There was a new design he'd wanted to try out on her tonight. With the aid of two hooks in the ceiling, the pattern would have looked like Cassie had wings when he was done with it—like a heavenly angel. But now all he had were the memories of their past time together—for once in his life, he didn't think it was enough.

———

Get *Knot a Chance* today!

Life is good—until it comes crashing down around him…

US Coast Guard Lieutenant Commander Stefan Lundquist exercises complete control in all things—professionally and personally. As a Shibari expert, he creates beautiful works of art on women's bodies with his ropes. But he makes sure they understand that their physical relationship has an expiration date.

Cassandra Myers knows she has to abide by Stefan's rules, but when she falls for him, she refuses to sign another contract and asks him to remove her collar, knowing her love is unrequited. Despite her anguish, she tries to move forward, focusing on her job as a cardiac rehabilitation tech and going to nursing school.

When Cassandra discovers her new patient is none other than the man she can't stop thinking about, she's determined to help him recover while trying to hide her feelings and protect her own broken heart.

But Stefan's new lease on life has him realizing how short his time on earth could be. Can he convince Cassandra he now wants more than a temporary arrangement, or has he lost her forever?

OTHER BOOKS BY SAMANTHA COLE

***Denotes titles/series that are only available on select digital sites. Paperbacks and audiobooks are available on most book sites.

THE TRIDENT SECURITY SERIES

Leather & Lace

His Angel

Waiting For Him

Not Negotiable

Topping The Alpha (MM)

Watching From the Shadows

Whiskey Tribute

Tickle His Fancy

No Way in Hell: A Steel Corp/Trident Security Crossover (co-authored with J.B. Havens)

Absolving His Sins

Option Number Three (MMF)

Salvaging His Soul

Trident Security Field Manual

Torn In Half

Burning For Him

*****Heels, Rhymes, & Nursery Crimes Series**

(with 13 other authors)

Jack Be Nimble: A Trident Security-Related Short Story

*****The Deimos Series**

Handling Haven: Special Forces: Operation Alpha

Cheating the Devil: Special Forces: Operation Alpha

The Trident Security Omega Team Series

Mountain of Evil

A Dead Man's Pulse

Forty Days & One Knight

The Doms of The Covenant Series

Double Down & Dirty (MFM)

Entertaining Distraction

Knot a Chance

Finding His Forever (MM)

Reclaiming His Soulmate

The Blackhawk Security Series

Tuff Enough

Blood Bound

Master Key Series

Master Key Resort

Master Cordell

HAZARD FALLS SERIES

Don't Fight It (MMF)

Don't Shoot the Messenger (MFM)

Don't Burn Bridges

THE MALONE BROTHERS SERIES

Her Secret

Her Sleuth

Her Savior

LARGO RIDGE SERIES

Cold Feet

*****ANTELOPE ROCK SERIES**

(CO-AUTHORED WITH J.B. HAVENS)

Wannabe in Wyoming

Wistful in Wyoming (M/M)

COCK & BULL SERIES (M/M)

Scout

Rico

STANDALONES

Where the Broken Bloom

ABOUT SAMANTHA COLE

USA Today Bestselling Author Samantha Cole is a retired police officer and paramedic who now writes heart-pounding romance in multiple forms—MF, MM, and ménage. From military heroes to rugged cowboys and small-town heat, her stories blend passion, loyalty, and danger in perfect balance.

Awards:

Wannabe in Wyoming (co-authored by J.B. Havens) won the bronze medal in the 2021 Readers' Favorite Awards in the General Romance category.

Scattered Moments in Time won the gold medal in the 2020 Readers' Favorite Awards in the Fiction Anthology category.

Where the Broken Bloom (formerly *The Road to Solace)* won the silver medal in the 2017 Readers' Favorite Awards in the Contemporary Romance category.

Sexy Six-Pack's Sirens Group on Facebook
Website: www.samanthacolebooks.com
Newsletter: samanthacolebooks.com/mailing-list

facebook.com/SamanthaColeAuthor

instagram.com/samanthacoleauthor

bookbub.com/profile/samantha-a-cole

goodreads.com/SamanthaCole

amazon.com/Samantha-A-Cole/e/B00X53K3X8

tiktok.com/@samanthacoleauthor

youtube.com/@SamanthaACole-bp6yu

www.ingramcontent.com/pod-product-compliance
Lightning Source LLC
Chambersburg PA
CBHW071930190726
48293CB00004B/1226